LOVE REMEMBERED

Nadine told herself it would be different with Lawrence this time.

She had been little more than a college girl when he had introduced her to the power of passion. But that had been four years ago—and since then she had come a long way. Now when she gave herself to him, it would be different. They were two adults who knew the score.

Then she was in Lawrence's arms again, and as he slowly undressed her and skillfully began to caress her with his artist's touch, his artist's sensitivity, she *really* knew the score . . . she knew that once again there could be no limits to her love. . . .

ELLIE WINSLOW had a romantic upbringing traipsing all over the world, including several years spent in Italy where *Painted Secrets* is partially set. In addition to writing, Ellie enjoys playing music and reading. She lives in New York's Greenwich Village.

Dear Reader:

The editors of Rapture Romance have only one thing to say—thank you! At a time when there are so many books to choose from, you have welcomed ours with open arms, trying new authors, coming back again and again, and writing us of your enthusiasm. Frankly, we're thrilled!

In fact, the response has been so great that we now feel confident that you are ready for more stories which explore all the possibilities that exist when today's men and women fall in love. We are proud to announce that we will now be publishing four titles each month, because you've told us that two Rapture Romances simply aren't enough. Of course, we won't substitute quantity for quality! We will continue to select only the finest of sensual love stories, stories in which the passionate physical expression of love is the glorious culmination of the entire experience of falling in love.

And please keep writing to us! We love to hear from our readers, and we take your comments and opinions seriously. If you have a few minutes, we would appreciate your filling out the questionnaire at the back of this book, or feel free to write us at the address below. Some of our readers have asked how they can write to their favorite authors, and we applaud their thoughtfulness. Writers need to hear from their fans, and while we cannot give out addresses, we are more than happy to forward any mail.

Happy reading!

Robin Grunder
Rapture Romance
New American Library
1633 Broadway
New York, NY 10019

PAINTED
SECRETS

by
Ellie Winslow

RAPTURE ROMANCE

NEW AMERICAN LIBRARY

TIMES MIRROR

PUBLISHER'S NOTE

This novel is a work of fiction. Names, characters, places, and incidents either are the product of the author's imagination or are used fictitiously, and any resemblance to actual persons, living or dead, events, or locales is entirely coincidental.

Copyright © 1983 by Winslow Eliot

All rights reserved

SIGNET, SIGNET CLASSIC, MENTOR, PLUME, MERIDIAN and NAL BOOKS
are published by The New American Library, Inc.,
1633 Broadway, New York, New York 10019

First Printing, September, 1983

1 2 3 4 5 6 7 8 9

PRINTED IN THE UNITED STATES OF AMERICA

Chapter One

~~

"This is the operator. What number are you calling?"

"Long distance, please, to Florence, Italy."

"One moment. I'll get you the international operator."

While she waited for her call to be put through, Nadine gazed sightlessly at the cluttered piles of papers and catalogues on her desk, her heart pounding. The far-off ringing at the other end of the line transported her to the high-ceilinged, sparsely furnished room in the Florentine villa where the chunky black telephone used to be kept. Had the room changed much? she found herself wondering. Had Lily moved the telephone?

"Hello?"

The low, resonant voice ripped through the thousands of miles of telephone wire and into her fragile psyche. It could have been yesterday that she had seen him. Why, oh why had circumstances forced her to speak to him again?

But not a trace of her inward anguish was evident in her cool, crisp voice.

"Lawrence Stebbing, please."

There was a short, surprised silence, and Nadine wondered if he had already recognized her voice.

"This is Lawrence."

She swallowed another gulp of emotion that threatened to show itself in her voice and said hastily:

"This is Nadine Barnet. Everett Mills has no doubt informed you that I am the exhibition coordinator at the Mills Gallery and am responsible for arranging your show this fall."

"Nadine?" Lawrence sounded amazed. "Is that really you?"

"Nadine Barnet," she repeated. "I work at the Mills Gallery."

She heard him take a breath.

"Everett didn't tell me. How are you, Nadine?"

She was angry at him for asking that question, but she was angrier at herself for discovering she still had not overcome her bitterness. Simply hearing his voice stirred up muddy clouds of antagonism in her thumping chest.

"Mr. Mills wishes me to pay you a visit to discuss which paintings will be included in the exhibition. I need to find out when such a trip would be convenient for you."

"Nadine!" Lawrence exclaimed, and she knew he was irritated by her pretense of their being strangers. He controlled himself, however. "You're coming to Florence? Everett did say he was sending somebody but didn't tell me who." He paused. "Any time's fine with me. When can you come?"

"How about Monday? The sooner I get this aspect of the show organized the sooner I can move on to other matters I have to deal with."

"Monday's fine." He sounded disappointed at her lack of enthusiasm at the prospect of seeing him again, she thought with satisfaction. "How are you, Nadine?" he asked again. "It's a wonderful surprise to hear your voice."

"Mr. Mills believes this trip is necessary," she replied frostily, "and I couldn't persuade him otherwise." She felt a wicked glee inside her at the power she now had over her once-violent emotions. She would let him know how she had changed! Never more would he be able to create feelings of passionate jealousy, fury, and desire in her, as though she were one of his freshly stretched canvases ready for the hard, bold strokes from his brush. She was in control now, and the realization exhilarated her. She kept her voice cool. "He isn't aware of the fact that we used to know each other. It's purely a coincidence that I've been assigned this task, and I'm counting on our both forgetting our past—uh—acquaintance."

The silence was uncomfortably long. Finally Lawrence said:

"Give me a call when you arrive in Florence and we'll get together right away." His tone was civil; she could read nothing into it. "Do you know where you'll be staying?"

Not with him, he could be sure of that!

"The Continental Hotel. I'll call you from there on Monday."

Again a silence. Could he hear the rapid hammering in her chest?

"I'm looking forward to seeing you again," he said.

He would know how little she cared! She clenched the receiver and replied in a neutral tone:

"I'm looking forward to seeing you and your wife, too."

Her eyes closed tightly and she was enveloped by the safety of darkness. Had she angered or irritated or hurt him by her indifference? Again that strange, newly discovered power over her emotions elated her. Never again would he have the chance to hurt her, her heart cried in relief. She would be armed at their next encounter, and her weapon would be the wisdom of experience.

But she was disconcerted when he made no direct reply.

"Goodbye then, Nadine. Talk to you next week."

It took her a full five minutes of wrestling with churning hostility, elation, and guilt before she felt controlled enough to go to Everett Mills's office and report to him the outcome of the conversation. She pushed her thick, light-brown hair away from her wide forehead in a gesture of sudden weariness, and knocked on the closed door.

"Come in."

Everett was sitting behind his fake-leather desk, his feet

resting on a pile of catalogues, talking loudly into the telephone. His bloodshot, pale blue eyes, sandwiched between heavy, yellowish lids and bruise-colored under-eye pouches, examined her speculatively. He waved toward the armchair without ceasing to talk belligerently into the mouthpiece. Nadine took the chair and lost herself in her memories.

Florence! It had been over four years since she was there, and in just a few days she would actually be in the exquisite city again, walking on the familiar streets, immersed in the golden light, smelling the fragrances of mingled fresh coffee, homemade wine and olive oil, hearing the language she once knew well. Her yearning to see the city again was equal to her aversion to seeing Lawrence, but aside from a visit or two to his studio in order to select the paintings for the exhibition, and a meeting to discuss business details, there would be no need to spend much time with him. She wished she could take Jamie with her. Young as he was, she was certain her four-year-old son would love Florence.

"You're in a bit of a daze, aren't you?" Everett's raspy voice reached her sharply, and she realized he had been talking to her for some time.

She forced herself to pay attention to her employer. He was a heavyset, balding man of about fifty, feared and disliked by most of his staff because of his arrogance and hot temper. But he had always been particularly fond of Nadine, had even paid for her classes at Columbia. Getting her master's degree while supporting herself had presented almost insurmountable difficulties, and while the tuition money hadn't solved all her problems, it had been a great help. In return for his generosity, Everett wanted Nadine to go out with him, but she had always firmly refused.

"I've made arrangements with Mr. Stebbing to fly to Italy on Monday, as you requested," she informed him.

Everett lit a cigarette and blew out the match with fat, pursed lips. A laugh choked him.

"Was our friend happy to hear from you?"

She raised a feathery eyebrow coolly. "I don't know why he'd care one way or the other. The show has already been scheduled. We simply have to decide which paintings we'll show, and what prices we'll ask. He knows that."

"Naturally, sweets. But didn't Stebbing express any delight at all at hearing from you? I expected surprise at the very least."

Nadine's expressionless, oval face turned a little pale, but she tried to shrug indifferently. What did Everett know? She stood up: It was past five o'clock already and she had to pick up Jamie from her sister Charlotte's.

Everett waved the cigarette through the air, already bluish with smoke, and his jeweled ring on a pudgy forefinger flashed. It was unbearably stuffy inside the office.

"I'm very pleased you're already acquainted with Stebbing," he continued carelessly. "It'll make this entire project a hell of a lot easier. I'm trusting you not to let him get away with anything—you know he has a reputation for being very difficult to work with."

Nadine sat down again.

"You're mistaken." Her voice was not just cool now; it was colder than ice. "I don't know him."

Another grating laugh filled the small room. Everett drew on the cigarette before replying. "I don't see any reason why you have to lie to me, dear. I happen to be aware that you do not just 'know' Stebbing, but that you know him very intimately indeed."

Nadine was grateful she had steeled herself so often to pointed inquiries, indiscreet questions, and slanderous remarks before now; it made it possible to remain rigidly still and raise her eyebrow disdainfully. But her fear was real. How did Everett know about the relationship? What if he knew more than that? What if he knew—

"Why you'd want to deny a relationship with the famous Stebbing is beyond me." Everett shrugged his massive shoulders in amazement. "If you'd told me about it when I interviewed you for this job I wouldn't have asked to see your résumé.''

"Did Mr. Stebbing inform you that we had already met?" Nadine chose her words carefully.

Everett eyed her curiously. "No, of course not. Do you think he'd bother claiming to have slept with a nobody from nowhere? It's *your* silence that surprises me, sweetie.''

With an effort Nadine kept her temper, as she had learned to do over the course of the two years she had worked for Everett.

"I asked you how you learned that I'd met Mr. Stebbing." If a tone of voice could chill the atmosphere, the office would have had icicles hanging from the glossy white ceiling. But Everett seemed immune to the cold.

"You'll learn soon enough," he replied teasingly. "I only wish I could see your face when you do." He drew on the cigarette again, then stubbed it out in the black ashtray as though he were crushing an insect. "We have one or two matters that I want you to settle before Stebbing signs the contracts for the show. You'll be taking those with you. I'll leave the choice of paintings to your discretion, naturally, and to his. You have quite extraordinary judgment in these matters, and I trust you implicitly.''

She inclined her head slightly, acknowledging the compliment.

"But one thing, Nadine." There was always a motive behind any tribute Everett paid. "There's a painting of Stebbings' that's so superior to any of his other work that someone of your inexperience may not be able to judge its greatness. Therefore I'm going to have to insist that it is included in the exhibition in spite of how you may react to it.''

Was that glee she heard in his raspy, belligerent voice?

"Which painting is that?" she inquired politely.

"It's called *Tuscan Dawn*.''

"I'll remember." She rose again.

Everett looked disappointed at her indifference.

"Not one of the paintings you saw when you were involved with him, eh?"

"You're under a misapprehension regarding my acquaintance with Stebbing, I'm afraid. We did meet once, but we did not hit it off, and I doubt that he even remembers me by now. It was several years ago."

"Indeed?" Everett's dry amusement made her heart sink. Quickly she picked up her purse and said goodnight. "Free for dinner tonight?" His voice stayed her.

"No, I'm not." She opened the door. "Goodnight."

Everett let out an exaggerated sigh. "What did Lawrence have that I don't? It's beyond me."

"I'll see you tomorrow," Nadine said, escaping out the door. Hard as she tried she could not treat her boss's unwelcome flirtations lightly.

Once she was out on the street, Nadine turned toward Madison Avenue, swept into the lively current of rush-hour pedestrians. Because she was already late she took a bus uptown to her sister's, where Jamie was waiting. At the thought of Jamie her almond-shaped gray eyes softened. She loved Jamie with every ounce of passion she had once felt for his father. If Lawrence discovered Jamie's existence, what might happen? The possibilities made her shiver in spite of the heat. What if he wanted custody of her child? She hadn't the means to fight the famous, wealthy artist in court. The thought of being separated from her child was sickening. It was imperative that Lawrence not find out about his son.

The uptown bus was crowded, and when Nadine alighted on 86th street she was hot and tired. Beads of perspiration trickled down her wide brow, and the thought that she would soon be in Florence again, with its refreshing breezes and fragrant country air, lifted her spirits. Seeing Lawrence was the only gray blot on what otherwise would be a heavenly trip.

Charlotte opened the door and greeted her sister with an

affectionate kiss. Only two years separated them, and they shared the same brown hair and soft gray eyes. But there the resemblance ended. Married, with two children, Charlotte had an air of contentment bordering on complacency that both amused and exasperated her restless, more cynical younger sister. Whereas Nadine was slim almost to the point of thinness, Charlotte was plump and matronly, and it was sometimes difficult for Nadine to remember the weight-conscious, discontented teenager she had grown up with.

"Hello, dear. Jamie's in the kitchen." Charlotte closed the door behind them and led her sister through the luxurious living room to the perfectly clean, modern kitchen. A pleasant aroma of roast chicken wafted from the oven.

Jamie sat at the orange breakfast table drawing with colored crayons. He looked up at Nadine with three-cornered dark green eyes that never ceased to remind her of his father. His face lit up in joy and he submitted to her fierce embrace with a rare, tender smile on his serious face.

"Darling! Did you have a good day at school?"

"No. Mrs. Smith was mean."

"What'd she do?" Nadine kissed the top of his fair hair and wished for the thousandth time that he didn't have to go to kindergarten so young.

"Made my friend Ginny stand on her chair 'cause she was talking in class."

"That isn't such an awful punishment," Nadine said gently.

"But she wasn't talking." Jamie's sense of justice was already strong. "I was. But Mrs. Smith wouldn't let me stand on my chair."

Nadine reassured him sympathetically, then turned back to her patient sister.

"You're late today," Charlotte remarked. "Lots of work?"

Nadine nodded. "I'm exhausted."

"Let me fix you a drink. Something's happened, hasn't it?"

"Something's about to happen, anyway. Yes, I'd love a drink. Where are your kids?"

"Watching television, of course. I never seem to be able to get them out of the den except to eat. Jamie didn't want to join them, so he's been keeping me company." Charlotte handed her sister a glass of scotch and water. "Jamie, do you want to come into the living room with us?"

"I'll stay here," Jamie replied, immersed in his drawing again.

Nadine followed her sister into the living room and took off her jacket. Sighing, she stretched out on the sofa. The large, rectangular living room had always been a source of pleasure, for she had an instinctive eye for beauty. The combination of damask gold curtains, gilded light fixtures on white walls, and the light blue sofa, armchairs, and plush rug reminded her of Florence, which her memory had cloaked in colors of summer blue and sunshine gold.

"Tell me what happened at work," Charlotte said, curling up comfortably in a plump armchair opposite Nadine. "I hope it's not bad news. You look as though it might be."

"In a way it is." Nadine sighed again. "Everett has ordered me to go to Florence next week."

Charlotte sat up in the chair, her eyes wide.

"Nadine!" she shrieked. "That's wonderful!"

Glumly, Nadine said, "Is it? I'm going there to talk to Lawrence Stebbing about his upcoming exhibition at the Mills Gallery."

Charlotte sank back into her chair as though she had been struck.

"Oh, no."

"I didn't tell you we're planning to do a show of his work because I kept hoping it wouldn't come off. Lawrence has a knack for making the lives of people who run his exhibitions absolutely miserable. I was sure Everett would lose his temper and give up the idea. But it seems Lawrence has been quite amenable to the plans, so far. I'm to go over there and discuss which paintings we're going to show, prices, things like that.''

"Everett can't make you go, dear," Charlotte said firmly. "Tell him you can handle the details over the phone.''

"You can be sure I tried my damndest to persuade him not to send me. Other than quitting, I don't have a choice. And I can't quit, not unless I have some other job.''

There was a silence while the sisters looked at each other.

"He'll be coming to New York for the show, then?'' Charlotte asked at last. She was not talking about Everett.

Nadine nodded.

"You'll have to tell him about Jamie, then.''

"No!'' Nadine replied fiercely. "He mustn't find out, ever!''

Charlotte was silenced by Nadine's vehemence.

"I can leave Jamie with you, can't I, while I'm gone? I don't plan to be away more than three or four nights.''

"Of course Jamie can stay here.'' She hesitated. "Are you sure you've thought of everything that might get you out of going on this trip, though? You must hate the thought of seeing him again.''

Nadine's voice was low. "I do hate it. It'll be hell. But I don't have a choice. You know I can't quit my job.''

"No, you can't do that,'' Charlotte said, her face troubled.

"Don't worry about me.'' Nadine managed a smile. "I was just a kid when we were together last. I'm all grown up now. He won't affect me.''

"But you just said it would be hell.''

Nadine finished her scotch with a gulp.

"Hell's a state of mind,'' she said with a forced laugh. "And the gates to my mind will be locked as soon as I get off that plane. I'll be okay. Really, Char, I don't care about him anymore. Believe me.''

"I can't.'' Her sister's voice was small. "He hurt you so badly. He cheated on you, lied to you, and left you with a child. And I know how you loved him.''

Nadine's hands clasped each other. "Loved him is right, Char. I did love him. But I don't anymore. He's nothing to me now, and he never will be again. Besides"—her eyelids fluttered downward to hide the pain from her sister—"he's married now."

"Married!" It was a gasp.

Nadine shrugged. "Don't sound so shocked. You're married yourself."

"When did you find out?"

"Oh, some time ago. About a year after I came back to the States." Still she did not raise her eyes. She would never forget the anguish she had experienced on learning about Lawrence's marriage to Lily. "One of his artist friends mentioned it at an art opening I happened to attend."

"You never told me!" Charlotte said reproachfully.

Nadine tried to smile at the concern in her sister's voice. "I felt too humiliated then. But honestly, I'm over it now. I'll be gone only a few days, and nothing can happen in a few days." She finished her drink, rose, and went over to pat her sister's shoulder. "I'm going to take Jamie home for some dinner. Thanks for looking after him." She disappeared into the kitchen.

Charlotte accompanied them to the front door. "I won't get any sleep tonight trying to think of a way to get you out of going on this trip," she told Nadine. "Everett can't force you to go!"

"You don't know Everett," Nadine replied. "But let me know if you come up with anything."

Hand in hand with Jamie, she set off down the hall to the elevator.

Chapter Two

Nadine had met him almost five years ago. She had just graduated from Vassar, with a B.A. in Art History. Her parents offered her a trip to Italy as a graduation present. For two months Nadine wandered from city to city, her rucksack on her back, staying at youth hostels and cheap bed-and-breakfast places, stingily eking out the small allowance her parents gave her in order to make the trip last as long as possible. She quickly fell in love with Italy; she was overwhelmed by the art treasures and enraptured by the friendly people, and she adored the language, which she soon learned.

She had already visited Florence once, when she first arrived in Italy, but before returning to the United States she went back to visit the city she loved best of all one more time. She stayed at the large, rambling youth hostel near Fiesole, and spent her last week in the museums and churches or simply wandering the exquisite streets and exploring the piazzas and sidewalk cafés, dreaming of someday returning to the city to live.

Her flight to New York was scheduled to leave from Rome the following day; the youth hostel where she was staying was booked solid for the weekend, so even if she had had enough money to stay over another night—which she did not—there would have been no room for her. She had just enough money for the train to take her to Rome, and one night in the Rome youth hostel. With any luck, they would feed her on the airplane, she thought ruefully, looking longingly at a *gelateria* from which several teenagers were emerging licking ice cream cones. Never mind—her mother would feed her enough to make up for the entire two months when she arrived back home.

She was on her way to the train station, already late, taking in with delight and sadness combined her last sights of Florence. Ominous clouds gathered on the horizon. The heat foretold a thunderstorm. There was a strange, vibrant electricity in the air that made her feel uneasy and excited, despite her imminent departure from the city she loved.

Large, clear raindrops began to fall heavily from the black clouds that suddenly darkened the streets. In a moment the little street was deserted. People huddled in doorways and fled into stores to wait for the cloudburst to pass. Thunder clapped loudly overhead.

Ordinarily, Nadine would have joined the people crowded in the doorways and chattering excitedly about the storm, but she was in danger of missing the last train to Rome that day. So she hurried through the torrential rainfall, which seemed to grow heavier as she walked. Thick, muddy rivers began streaming down the gutters, and Nadine had to leap across wide puddles to reach the sidewalk.

She arrived at the train station. Anxiously she saw that she had less than a minute to get her ticket and jump on the train. She pushed her way through the milling crowds to the ticket counter. The ticket agent shook his head discouragingly when she told him she was trying to make the Rome train, and gave her the ticket with the information that she would have to take the following day's train, leaving at six in the morning.

Knowing that Italian trains almost never left on time, Nadine thanked him cheerfully, then whipped around to run toward the platform, only to crash headlong into a man who was hurrying toward the ticket counter to buy his ticket.

Her rucksack was dashed to the ground and its contents

spilled onto the wet, grimy station floor. Nadine lay sprawling, and a crowd quickly gathered around her to make sure she was all right. She assured the people she was, but could not restrain a cry when the man who had knocked her over put his hand on her elbow to help her up.

Tears of pain filled her eyes. "You're hurt," he said, in English. He looked at her with concern and impatience, his brow creased in a frown.

Nadine shook her head. "It's just my elbow. I'll be okay." She managed to stand up, not without another grimace of pain.

The stranger glanced at his watch, gave a barely perceptible shrug, then turned his attention to her elbow.

"It looks sprained. We'd better get you to a doctor."

"Oh, no!" Nadine objected. How on earth would she be able to pay for a doctor? "I'll be fine. It's more important that I try and make my train."

The man quickly picked up the scattered belongings and shoved them back in her rucksack. "Which train is that?" he asked. "I'll carry this for you."

"To Rome. I hope it's been delayed."

The stranger grinned at her. He had a disarming, slightly crooked smile that made Nadine respond with her own lovely smile without thinking.

"That's the one I was trying to make too," he said. "I'm afraid we've both missed it. And it's my fault for running into you like that. I'm so sorry. The next one isn't till tomorrow morning."

He was struck by the dismayed look on her face. "Oh, no!" she exclaimed, again, more urgently.

"That bad, eh? What happens if you don't get to Rome tonight?"

Nadine tried to collect her wits. "My plane to New York leaves at noon. If I take the six-o'clock train tomorrow I guess I'll be able to make it." But where would she spend the night?

"Where will you stay tonight?" The stranger seemed to read her mind. "I have my car in the parking lot. Can I offer you a lift to your hotel?"

Nadine shook her head. She couldn't possibly afford a hotel, and the youth hostel was fully booked. She supposed she could sleep in the station waiting room. It was a dismal thought, but seeing the rain still pouring down outside, she decided it was the only course she could take.

"No, thanks. It really wasn't your fault, and you've missed your train now as well so I should be just as sorry for you."

"But what will you do? Are you sure you don't want a doctor to look at your arm?"

"I'm absolutely positive," she replied firmly. "Don't worry about me. I'll stick around here, I think."

The man frowned. "For the night? That's not a good idea."

She shrugged, and grimaced again as she tried to lift the rucksack onto her back.

"I'll be okay," she said lightly, trying not to be disconcerted by the stranger's penetrating gaze.

The man seemed to be weighing something in his mind. He obviously was not prepared to let her disappear into the smoky waiting room for the night.

"Look here," he said abruptly. "Since I've missed the train too I'll be going back to my house for the night and getting the train first thing in the morning too. Why don't you come back with me—I'd like to bandage up your arm at least, and in some way make up for my clumsiness in knocking you down. I'll make absolutely sure we're both on the six-o'clock train for Rome."

Nadine hesitated. Up till now she had not accepted any offers from people she had met who wanted her to stay with them. But this was different. The man was an American, for one thing, and he was definitely not flirting with her. He seemed genuinely remorseful. Besides, the thought of trying to get some sleep on the hard wooden seats in the railway station was a depressing one.

"It's my fault you missed your train," he added, flashing his crooked grin again. "The least you can do is let me try to make amends."

Nadine replied at last, "I don't really have much of a choice, or else I'd never take advantage of your very kind offer, but, thank you. I—"

"Good," the stranger interrupted her impatiently. "Let me carry that, will you? My car's this way."

Through the heavy rain they ran toward a white Fiat parked by a crumbling brick wall. Thunder crashed down overhead and lightning crackled in the sky, and again Nadine was enveloped by her earlier sense of euphoria. It was as though she were embarking on a wonderful adventure that she had been looking forward to for years and years. She slid into the front seat next to her rescuer and offered him another lovely smile.

"My name's Nadine," she told him.

"And I'm Lawrence. Is your door locked? We're off, then."

They spoke very little on the drive. Lawrence had to squint through the thick rain flowing down the windshield, the slow wipers doing little to help. Covertly, Nadine glanced at her companion. He was younger than she at first supposed; not much over thirty. His nose was the most striking aspect to his profile: It dipped between his narrow-set eyes, then jutted out angularly to thin, high nostrils at the end. She suspected his forehead was wide, but it was covered with a shock of dark brown hair, and heavily creased with a frown of concentration as he scanned the slick road ahead. His cheeks were gaunt, freshly shaved, with two jagged creases running down toward a determined jaw. He glanced over and caught her examination of his features. Unembarrassed, she met his very dark green eyes with her own clear ones, then as he looked back at the road she did also, feeling strangely excited.

A thin yellow band of light running along the horizon illuminated the darkened, soaked countryside in an eerie glow. The cloudburst passed; the thunder groaned in the distance, heading north. But the storm seemed to have left its electricity behind, Nadine thought, feeling as though her skin would send off tiny sparks were this man to touch her. She studied the hands that held the steering wheel with casual concentration. The fingers were long and tapered at the ends. Patches of brown hair above the knuckles and creeping just beyond the cuffs of his herringbone jacket outlined the sinewy muscles and blue veins running along the back of his hands. What did she sense in those hands that sent a tremor of excitement through her? She did not know. They were strange, masculine hands, quite unlike her slim, soft ones, so why did they seem familiar? More than familiar, in fact: Nadine was aware of a vague possessive feeling toward those hands. She looked away again and gazed out the window.

A narrow road wound up a hill, bound by rain-soaked hedges and tufts of glistening grass on either side. He pulled the car up onto a grassy shoulder and switched off the engine. Nadine looked around, wondering where they were.

"It's across the street," the man said, reading her thoughts again. "We'll have to run for it."

She nodded and opened the car door. It was still raining, although not as heavily. Lawrence tilted up his collar, reached for her wet rucksack, and got out first, sprinting across the gray pavement to a tiny gate buried in the thick shrubbery. Nadine followed.

The narrow stone-flagged path, bordered by untended yellow rose bushes, led them through a wild tangle of blackberry bushes, tall grasses, and a baby pine tree, to an unkempt lawn. Whatever Lawrence's talents were, gardening was not one of them, Nadine thought to herself. But there was a magic to the rain-bright leaves, the sparkling tall grass, even the mud that spilled out between the gray-brown stones in the pathway.

Nadine follwed him around the side of the lawn and came upon the villa, tall and thin and shell-pink in a sudden ray of sun that slid to earth between the low, thick clouds. The first sight of Lawrence's home made her stop dead in her tracks. Not even the silver rain falling lightly down the back of her neck and easing its way through her already soaked cotton sweater and jeans broke the spell.

"Come on in," Lawrence called from the unpainted oak door. She joined him, feeling foolishly overenthusiastic.

The entire ground floor was one room, gleaming, brick-red tiles stretching smoothly away from the front door. On the right there was a compact kitchen area, fitted with wood cupboards, overlooking the front part of the house. On the other side of the square room were simple furnishings spaced around a fireplace: a low couch, two olive-green armchairs, and a low wood coffee table with some magazines lying carelessly on top. Large windows opened out on all four walls, but not one sign of neighboring habitats could be seen. On the far side of the room were glass doors leading onto a long, stone-walled patio overlooking a wide expanse of field and distant hills beyond. Nadine had never seen a house like this; she could not imagine anyone living in such a place.

Lawrence seemed unconscious of her awe. He swung her rucksack over one shoulder and headed for the marble staircase that wound up over the kitchen.

"First you'll take a hot bath," he told her unceremoniously. "I don't want to be responsible for your catching pneumonia as well as for spraining your elbow. Follow me."

The second floor was also only one large square room. Here a wide bed beneath one of the windows denoted Lawrence's sleeping quarters. The floor was pale hardwood. Apart from an austere, darkly varnished bureau, there was no other furniture. A bathroom had been partitioned off in one corner. It was large and luxuriously outfitted, with the longest bath Nadine had ever seen. Lawrence turned on the hot water, then turned his attention to her rucksack.

"Everything looks pretty sopping," he said ruefully. "We'll leave your things out to dry. Meantime you can borrow my robe—I'll leave it on my bed. And don't let the water out when you're through. There's barely enough hot water for one bath, and I want one too."

Nadine nodded dutifully and waited for him to close the door. Then she took a breath. What an adventure! She stripped quickly, finally realizing how thoroughly chilled she was, and sank into the bath with a sigh of ecstasy. Who was this man who had the most wonderful bath in the world, living in this austere yet lovely place, seemingly on the edge of the world? Remembering his warning about the hot water, she did not remain in long, but got out, toweled herself dry, and then cautiously peeped out the door to survey the dimly lit bedroom.

The robe was on the bed, as Lawrence had promised. Hugging the large, royal blue towel around her chest, she skipped over and put it on, then vigorously dried her hair. When it was only slightly damp, she glanced in the tall mirror on the wall next to the bathroom. She looked smaller than usual in the oversize maroon flannel dressing gown gathered in thick folds around her slim waist.

Lawrence was slicing tomatoes in the kitchen when she went downstairs.

"That was quick," he said appreciatively. "I'll take my turn. Make yourself at home. I've poured you some brandy— that'll warm you up. You haven't caught a chill, have you?" This last was said with concern.

She shook her head. "Oh, no. I feel great."

"I still want to bandage your elbow, though," he remembered.

"Have your bath first." She smiled at him. "It won't get any worse in the next half hour."

"I won't be that long," he replied, responding with a grin. "Here's your brandy." He handed her a plump, crystal brandy snifter, then headed upstairs, two at a time.

Left alone, Nadine wandered around the large room, sipping the warming drink, trying to get a clearer picture of her host. To her surprised delight the books on the low shelves consisted mostly of her own favorites: several art books, and some biographies of artists that she had read and reread when she had first immersed herself in art history. The records included her favorite composers and singers, too. Lifting her head from the collection, her gaze settled on a painting that hung directly over the expensive stereo. It was a rough-hewn landscape, bewilderingly beautiful in spite of its darkness and harsh lines. Nadine narrowed her eyes thoughtfully. She knew she hadn't seen the painting before, but somehow she seemed to recognize it.

She examined the barely legible signature. Ah—Stebbing. One of her favorite modern painters. What a coincidence that this man liked him too! She turned to the few other paintings on the walls. They were all by the same artist, and each was more strangely familiar and harshly beautiful then the last.

"What do you think of them?" Lawrence joined her, casually toweling his wet hair, wearing jeans and an old gray sweater. His feet were bare.

She turned to him. "They're marvelous," she replied sincerely. "I've never seen these paintings even in reproduction. You're awfully lucky to have them. He's one of my favorite artists."

"Who is?" He stopped toweling his hair and looked at her curiously.

"Lawrence Stebbing."

"You've heard of him?"

"Of course!" she answered indignantly, wondering at the quizzical disbelief in his eyes. Then she frowned. His name was Lawrence too. It couldn't possibly be . . . Her face flushed. "Lawrence—?"

"That's me," he responded lightly. "Now let's see about your arm and about dinner."

Her voice was low and amazed. "You're Lawrence Stebbing?"

"Yup," he replied cheerfully. "But if I don't get something to eat pretty soon I won't be for much longer. Come with me to the kitchen and tell me about yourself. How did you hear about me?"

All night long they talked, about each other, about themselves. For the first time in her life, Nadine met someone who grasped her ideas and flew with them, expanding her thoughts to the outer realms of consciousness. Art and artists became vivid and personal instead of merely fascinating. The art concepts she had formulated over the years became interwebbed with history, philosophy, and the development of the human soul. It was more than interesting; it was enlightening. Never before had she experienced this flood of illumination pouring through her as they talked and talked—and talked.

In the black, quiet hour before dawn they fell companionably silent to listen to a burst of clear melody that issued forth from a nightingale in the woods on the edge of the field. Lawrence was seated on the low stone wall and Nadine on the wide couch on the sheltered patio. The rain had stopped; the storm-battered clouds broke in the indigo sky overhead to expose occasional windswept stars. Lawrence drew on his cigarette, and the light illuminated his brooding face in a flare of orange glow. She glimpsed an unfamiliar expression in the shadowed sockets of his narrow-set eyes that thrilled her, and made her uneasy. The glow faded and he crushed out the cigarette in the wood ashtray beside him. He stood up, a tall, stretching silhouette against the ragged sky behind.

Suddenly Nadine was afraid. Something momentous was occurring, something she as yet had no words to describe. He came slowly toward her and held out his hands. She was compelled by something deep within her to give him hers. Pulling her to her feet, he stared down at her, but this time it was too dark and confusing even to imagine his expression.

Lawrence took her hands and brought them behind his back, then folded his arms around her shoulders. His mouth found hers, gentle yet insistent. She tried to respond as though she knew what she was doing, but fear paralyzed her. Her body went rigid.

"You're frightened," he said suddenly, drawing his mouth away. "Why?"

She dropped her head, feeling terribly young beside the famous, gifted, older man. She was not so naive as not to realize that Lawrence's experience with women had probably made him take for granted that she would sleep with him in return for letting her stay at his house. She closed her eyes in the dark. Could she do it? Wouldn't making love with Lawrence Stebbing be a glorious climax to the most wonderful night of her entire life? She would cherish the memory always, wouldn't she?

"Hey." A thumb and forefinger lifted her chin. She could detect puzzlement in his low, resonant voice, and something else she did not recognize. "The rain's stopped. Let's go for a walk and see what that bird over there is singing about. Want to?"

Her relief was mixed with puzzlement. Had she mistaken his desire for her? Or had he realized she was too young, too inexperienced? She could not stop her body from trembling.

"Sure." She was amazed at how light and relaxed her voice sounded. Was he aware of the boiling emotions simmering in her chest, making her weak with a watery heat? He released her chin, and she unconsciously hugged the dressing gown around her waist.

"I'll get my jeans." She turned to the house.

"You'll need a sweater too." He followed her. "You can wear one of mine. Want me to turn on the lights?"

And see her confusion? "No, I can see." It was true: Dim starlight fell on the pale staircase, making it gleam dully beneath her bare feet. Her jeans, hanging over the shower curtain rod, were still damp; so was her underwear. She had an off-white cotton skirt that was dry, however.

Lawrence handed her a large, soft wool sweater. "What about your shoes?"

"Still wet." Was he going to stand there while she dressed? To be sure, it was dark, but . . . "I have flip-flops."

"Your feet will get awfully wet. The grass is soaked and muddy, too, I bet."

He seemed determined to stay with her. Nadine did not want to appear prudish. She pulled the casual drawstring skirt over her legs and hips and drew the belt around her waist, then slipped out of Lawrence's dressing gown. Quickly she pulled the sweater over her head.

"Do you usually wear just the bare essentials like that?" Lawrence asked, his voice sounding peculiar.

"Sometimes," she admitted. She rarely wore a bra anyway, and tonight the feel of her bare legs and naked thighs under the thin skirt made her tremble with a sensuous excitement. She stepped into the rubber sandals and headed for the stairs.

Side by side they set off across the silvery field behind the villa, their feet squelching in the tall, wet grass, wild flowers brushing against their knees. Nadine curled her bare toes with pleasure in the cold, fresh mud.

The nightingale's song grew louder as they neared the grove of trees. With every note Nadine felt herself spinning higher and higher into the Florentine night sky, brushing her breast against the stars, communing with a heavenly passion that she had never imagined could exist on earth.

"Here's the stream." Lawrence stopped her when they reached a winding brook coursing its way by the woods. Silver-blue reflections danced over dark rocks. "Come this way."

His warm hand found hers, powerful, unyielding, comforting, and the touch seemed to dissolve the cold ground beneath her feet. What was happening to her?

"Here." He stopped on the bank less than a foot to the other side of the stream. Nadine could have flown across.

"No, wait." Lawrence stopped her. "Put one foot there,

and one here. Like this." And he wrapped his arms around her waist. They both stood with one leg on either bank, facing the shadowy woods. "Now," he said softly. "Listen."

She listened. The nightingale, exhausted perhaps, was taking a recess, and a dog that had barked earlier in the distance was silent too. She listened. There was only the sound of Lawrence's heartbeat, thumping heavily against her back, mingling with the sound of the stream which swelled and faded in a silver symphony through her night-sensitive ears.

"The stream?" she whispered. What was happening?

"Yes. Can you hear it going in one ear and out the other? It's like a meditation."

She closed her eyes, listening. It was so: The water bubbled into one ear and through her humming thoughts, cooling them, refreshing them, then poured out her other ear and floated into the soft night.

"Yes." She could think of nothing else to say.

"You're cold."

"No, I'm not."

"But you're shivering."

Ah. "Maybe a little." But it wasn't the cold. The flowing water had cleared her confused mind and left her with a pale dawning of what had in fact happened to her. She had fallen in love with Lawrence Stebbing. In a random, unexpected accident she had met the man who had won her independent young heart. The realization was so big, so awesome, that she felt weak. Slipping through Lawrence's surprised arms, she sank onto the wet grassy bank and let her feet fall into the cool water, washing away the mud of previous years, previous incarnations, previous eternities that she knew she had shared with this man. Did he feel it too? she wondered. This shattering knowledge that her life belonged to him, and his to her?

"Lovely Nadine," he murmured, kneeling behind her and placing his hands on her shoulders. "Do you know what you're doing to me?"

She waited, not moving as he kissed her exposed neck. His hands coursed down the front of her sweater to her stomach. Then they slipped under the too-large sweater and moved deliriously slowly to her bare breasts. She moaned softly.

"Let's go back," he whispered huskily, after a few minutes.

Without warning the nightingale broke into song again.

They did not go inside the house. At the edge of the patio, Nadine slipped her muddy feet out of the rubber thongs and willingly allowed herself to be enfolded in Lawrence's arms again, as he drew her down next to him on the low wide sofa. He had a delicious scent of fresh mud and wet grass clinging to him. His lips, deceptively soft and sweet, took firm possession of her own, as his hand roamed up her thighs and over the swell of her hips. The artist's hands she had admired before created now with her as their canvas. Stroking slowly and lightly, then with the strength of passion, he sketched her with lines of flame.

Long, delicious moments later, she lay back on the low wide sofa, and Lawrence gazed at her in the paling light of early morning.

"You are an extraordinary woman," he murmured, tracing her exposed legs and thighs with strong, deliberate fingers, lifting the sweater over her head and kissing her breasts. Then, reluctantly, as though he could not bear to break the contact between their flesh, he stood and removed his clothes.

At first, he was content only to renew their kisses, but soon his passion heightened and he sought the ultimate intimacy. Wanting him, longing for him, Nadine still could not suppress a soft cry of pain. Lawrence drew away, staring at her.

"Why didn't you tell me?" he asked quietly. "I had no idea."

Tears filled her eyes. He would not want her now. But he kissed them away.

"I'll try not to hurt you," he said gently. "But are you sure you want to do this?"

Bravely she nodded, brushing angrily at her betraying tears.

Lawrence lay beside her, caressing her delicately, as though opening a flower.

"You're so soft and you smell so heavenly," he murmured into her hair. "Does this feel good?"

She nodded wordlessly, amazed by the sensations his tender caress produced in her body. He was not satisfied with the nod. He tilted her chin and stared into her eyes. Nadine was unable to look away.

"Does it?" he repeated, then closed his mouth over hers without waiting for her reply. Her arms crept around his neck, her fingers meshed with his dark hair. His lips moved to her ear and throat.

"It feels good," she whispered. She wanted him, all of him, as she had never wanted a man before. Her hands strayed to his hips, and he groaned.

"You're driving me crazy!" he exclaimed hoarsely.

Needing more than his caresses, she murmured his name entreatingly. His breath was hot against her throat, then he lifted himself and parted her legs with his knee. Nadine strained her hips to meet him. The ecstatic fullness made her forget the pain. She gripped his shoulders, no longer anxious about her inexperience, no longer worried about pleasing him, but lost in the surge of extreme pleasure crusading through her.

"Oh, baby—" Lawrence was restraining himself with difficulty. His mouth was buried in her breasts. The waves grew higher, stronger, swirling through Nadine's bloodstream, sweeping her into another heaven. She neared the edge, not knowing what she would find beyond. Lawrence drew her back. There was something imminent that she could not dream of. She neared the edge again, overwhelmed by the force of the desire that carried her there.

"Slowly, baby, slowly . . ." Lawrence caressed her.

For a moment she glimpsed the vast infinity of release that spread before her. She longed to tumble over the edge of the precipice into that vast realm of infinite satisfaction; again Lawrence gently eased her back to safety.

"Please," she moaned. "Please, Lawrence—"

His control was breaking also. His breathing came faster, his grip tightened on her shoulders.

Nadine cried aloud again. She was being pushed off the edge of the cliff. She fell into oblivion in a soul-shattering explosion, tumbling in long, ecstatic shudders through the golden light. She stopped falling after a while, and instead floated serenely through the heavenly atmosphere, breathing deeply, carried along by the strength of Lawrence's arms still wrapped around her.

The sun broke out over the distant, dawn-purple hills. Nadine opened her eyes to the dazzle of the sunstruck spray of diamondlike raindrops settled thickly in the field. They had talked so much; now they were both silent. Lawrence's eyes, very close to hers, drank in her rapture. There were no words needed to share the wonder of such a moment.

Chapter Three

❧

As the days that followed melted into weeks, and the weeks into months, a burnished-gold autumn found Nadine still together with Lawrence, living in his villa; found them still talking thirstily as though unable to drink enough from the other's understanding of their hitherto private or misunderstood thoughts; found them both deeply, ecstatically in love.

Nadine became Lawrence's model, his muse, his inspiration. He delighted in her enthusiasm, her unabashed affection for him, and her passionate desire. She had been a half-opened blossom of promise; now she felt opened, a full-blown rose, a woman steeped in dreams and plans and emotions.

The love Nadine felt for Lawrence bordered on adoration. All he said, what he did, how he loved, was perfection in her eyes. That he was famous, wealthy, gifted, and handsome was a by-product of his inherent nature, the crux of her love. She loved his loud belly-laugh that lighted his deep-set eyes with a glow of green fire, she loved the amazing power of his hands that could create magic on his canvases and in her body. She worshiped those hands, worshiped the mind that guided them, worshiped the soul that inspired them.

When he suggested that she attend the *università* in the fall to begin work on her master's degree in Art History, she willingly fell in with the plan. When he arranged for her to see a gynecologist about getting a diaphragm, she went without question. And when he told her, in the very early stages of their living together, that he had no interest in a formal commitment, she agreed wholeheartedly that affairs should be unrestricting in order to be their most fulfilling. She did not analyze all the various implications of this assertion; as a hypothetical statement, however, it seemed to ring true.

Lawrence said that he valued his independence too highly to want to lose it in a relationship. Again, Nadine admired his independence and did not foresee the day when these assertions might directly conflict with her overpowering love for him. Nadine did not care about his independence, or her own. They were together, terribly happy together, deeply in love. What part independence played in a love like theirs she did not stop to wonder.

Living with Lawrence became as natural as breathing, and as necessary. Her parents stormed at her from across the Atlantic, angry and hurt at her decision to remain in a foreign country with a stranger. Lawrence encouraged her to try to make them understand the reason for her decision. The outcome of these talks and letters was that her parents agreed to continue to send her an allowance and to pay for her courses, but so grudgingly that Nadine declared herself sick of their culturally deprived home. She described with scorn the sterile suburban house in Connecticut where she had grown up, and, understanding very little about her upbringing, Lawrence accepted her rejection of her past and came to believe he had in truth rescued her from a stagnant world to which she felt no tie.

Consequently, when Nadine began to feel pangs of homesickness, a longing for her parent's gay affection and chatter, Lawrence ignored her turnaround from scorn to nostalgia, thinking that she would get over this stage too. His obliviousness to her feelings only made them stronger.

As Christmas drew near, the ache grew raw. Christmas had always been a special family holiday. She had warm, loving memories of the festive season, being with friends and relatives,

surrounded by good cheer, fun parties, secrets, surprises, all
adding to the flurry of activity and excitement. When she
tried to describe this to Lawrence, he was contemptuous.
Christmas as a religious holiday was only slightly less ridiculous than Christmas as a materialistic holiday. He wanted no
part of either of them.

It was their first serious rift. Nadine grew morose and
irritable as the December days closed in; Lawrence ignored
her increasingly difficult moods. He suggested that she
go home for Christmas, as her parents begged that she do, but
Nadine could not bear to be parted from him even for two
weeks. She wanted to spend Christmas with Lawrence, to
make it a meaningful, special day, celebrating their love. But
Lawrence dogmatically refused to celebrate Christmas in any
way. The idea of celebrating their love was pretentious, he
argued. They celebrated that every day. Neither could gain the
other's understanding, as they used to in the early days of
their relationship; every argument nudged them farther apart
in their views.

They began quarreling about small, unimportant things.
Nadine took offense at the slightest pretext; in response Lawrence left her alone more frequently. The irritating quarrels
became fights; the fights became vicious battles, ending with
Lawrence striding out the door and slamming it behind him
with such violence that the villa shook. Where he went for
those long, miserable hours that Nadine was left alone she did
not know, and Lawrence refused to be questioned.

After a particularly acrid lashing-out one afternoon, Lawrence stormed out of the house, and Nadine, unable to bear
the thought of sitting around waiting for his return, took the
long walk into the city to try to fill in the hours. She was
walking along a wide street, hardly looking at the street
vendors and their various wares, when she noticed Lawrence
across the street sitting at a sidewalk café with another woman.
In a bewildering revelation she realized that all the hours he
spent away from the villa were probably shared with this

blond beauty—or perhaps some other woman—while she sat miserably at home waiting. She stared at his companion. Tall, vivacious, bubbling with gaiety, the woman leaned intimately against Lawrence, teasing his arm with the side of her cashmere-hugged breast. Her eyes sparkled, her high cheekbones were pink with happiness, her wide, generous lips sexily red. She was everything that the moody, homesick Nadine had not been the past month. As she stared at the strange woman, a bruise-colored cloud of jealousy seeped through her pores. She was unable to move.

Eventually the couple rose to leave. Lawrence wrapped his arm around the woman's bright yellow sweater; she slipped an arm around his waist. She was tall; she was gorgeous; she was mature. Even from across the road Nadine was enthralled by her dizzying, commanding presence. They headed toward the Arno, away from Lawrence's villa.

Nadine did not follow. She turned, dry-eyed, stunned, hopelessly alone, toward home. She knew she should leave him, but the thought made her shudder. She had forgotten how to live without Lawrence.

For several hours after she returned she sat upstairs on the edge of the wide bed, her arms clasped around her cold chest, waiting. Well after dark the front door slammed shut. He found her, motionless, in the bedroom.

"Are you okay?" he asked.

If he was going to be sweet to her she could not bear it. Choking on tears that refused to flow, she said accusingly, "Where were you?"

He seemed taken aback by her sharp tone. "I don't have to tell you that."

"No, you don't." Her voice was needle-thin. "I saw you."

He raised an indifferent eyebrow.

"Who was she?" she insisted.

"Her name's Lily," he replied coldly, taking off his jacket in irritation. "I've been seeing her on and off for the past five years. Unlike you, I don't drop all my own pursuits at the drop of a hat."

"You call Lily a pursuit and our love a drop of a hat?" she said furiously. Her neck was rigid, her shoulders stiff.

"She's a friend."

"A friend! She didn't look like a friend to me!"

He came over to her. "Nadine." He spoke gently but firmly. "We've gone over this before. We're not tied to each other. We agreed to that, remember? I don't want to have a scene like this every time I go off on my own."

"You weren't on your own today!"

He grew exasperated. "You're behaving like a spoiled child. This sort of thing is exactly the reason why I don't like to get involved in relationships. There are no restrictions to our affair, remember? You're just as free to go off with whoever you'd like as I am."

Nadine was obstinate. "Being free to screw whoever you want isn't the same as actually doing it. I'm willing to live on the assumption that we're both free, but I can't accept that you'd take advantage of that freedom."

"Then you're hypocritical."

Her voice was low with desperation. "I'm not being hypocritical. If you love someone, you don't want anyone else."

Lawrence folded his arms and looked down at her. "You sometimes make it very difficult for me to love you," he returned slowly.

There was a sudden contraction in her chest, making it difficult for her to breathe. She stood up weakly, unable to bear the implication of what he'd said.

"I'm not saying I don't love you, damm it!" he exclaimed. "I do; you know I do. I'm just saying you're impossible to get along with sometimes. I am too."

She shook her head blindly. "If you really love someone you don't go off with someone else as soon as things aren't perfect between you. Love implies loyalty, understanding, and a responsibility to try and work things out. You won't take that responsibility. You won't accept the fact that there are more parts to love than making love and having a good time together."

"Nicely profound." He retired to the low windowsill, his legs stretched out, his arms folded. "I'd say love also implies trust, which includes not jumping to conclusions about the other person's friendships." His dark eyes narrowed.

She felt utterly alienated from him; he did not understand this hammering, horrible jealousy that stripped her of all logic. Her voice shook.

"You can be sarcastic if you like, but don't be too sure there aren't some things I know about better than you. You might be gifted and famous and rich, but you don't know the first thing about love if you can let down the woman you say you love this easily."

"Melodrama doesn't suit you, sweetheart." he replied tiredly. "You've sentenced me without a hearing, you've worked yourself up into a passion for no reason, and you top it all by saying I don't know what love is."

"You don't," she replied stubbornly.

He stood up abruptly, annoyed. "I'll show you what love is, you self-righteous brat." He began unbuttoning his shirt.

As the cherished weave of dark hair on his chest came into view, Nadine felt sick to her stomach, thinking of Lily's long red fingernails running through it, teasing it, playing with it. Nadine willed her legs to take her to the stairs.

He caught her wrist with one hand; the other continued unbuttoning his shirt. "Where are you going?"

The pain of contact was too much to bear. Fiercely she jerked her wrist from his grip and clasped the bruised flesh.

"I wish I could make you understand." Why did she find it so hard to breathe? "But I can't. You don't *want* to understand." She stared at the taut lips Lily had kissed, at his hostile face that had smiled at Lily, then dropped her eyes. "The thought of sleeping with you tonight makes me sick."

She turned, half stumbling, and went down the stone flight of stairs.

That had been one of the many times she had sought solace by the stream where Lawrence had first taken her. She lay face-down, her head leaning over the edge of the bank, the tips of her hair brushing the running water, her eyes closed. But tonight even the silvery gurgles of the brook did not alleviate the rising hysteria that spilled onto the wet, cool grass which she pounded with her small, ineffectual fists.

Lawrence found her there at last and took her back to the house without speaking. He put her to bed and held her in his arms, warming her chilled body without desire, without passion

After that night, things worsened steadily. The fact that Lawrence tried to make light of his infidelity only increased Nadine's pent-up resentment, and she exploded at unexpected, inconvenient moments, infuriating Lawrence. He spent more time away from the villa when he wasn't in his third floor studio painting. Each time he left Nadine brooded or raged or wept, and by the time he returned her jealousy would have reached feverish heights. If she didn't lash out she was sullen and withdrawn. Lawrence tried to pretend indifference to her varying moods, hoping she would stop behaving badly when she saw she was not affecting him. But his indifference was like a nightmarish straitjacket: It gave her no opportunity to vent her anger and no opening to resolve their conflicts.

The final straw occurred on Christmas Eve, a night on which Nadine still cherished a hope that Lawrence would surprise her with the intimate celebration she craved. If he did, she would grant him amnesty, for she felt ungovernably homesick that day. She tried to keep her mind off the activities her family were up to, occupying herself with shopping for champagne and groceries to prepare an elaborate meal, certain that Lawrence would be touched by her effort toward a reconciliation. When she returned to the villa he had gone out, but her optimism persuaded her that he was probably planning his own surprise for her.

She built a fire in the hearth, lit fresh red candles on the mantel, and set the dining table prettily. She wore a new red angora sweater, black slacks, and an exquisite coral necklace Lawrence had bought her a month earlier.

But why had she imagined he might change his mind about celebrating Christmas with her? The hours crawled. She read a book, overcooked the roasting turkey, blew out the candles at last before they expired completely, and waited. And waited.

Impatience turned to annoyance, annoyance to anger, anger to jealousy, jealousy to grief, and grief to blind rage. She was utterly spent when Lawrence finally returned after midnight— with Lily. Both were thoroughly drunk, laughing hysterically, and to Nadine's blistering eyes, constantly touching each other. They tried to get Nadine to join in their joking and laughter, as they would a peevish six-year-old, she thought, but they gave up in the face of her icy responses. That was the last time she had visited the stream for solace, returning only when she heard the car drive away. Thinking she was alone again, she walked slowly back to the patio, her heart crushed in the pain of humiliation and grief at the dreaded end of her affair with Lawrence. Up till now, Nadine would have forgiven him everything if he had asked. But no longer. Not another night would she spend in his house. She should have left weeks ago; only a pathetic optimism had kept her at his side.

Lawrence stood on the patio. He was still drunk, but tried to apologize. "It was a bad idea. I thought you'd like a party—"

She walked past him without speaking. The acrid smell of burned turkey filled the house, mingling with overdone plum cake. She didn't care. Seeing the elegantly set table, the almost-burned-out candles, and the champagne glasses waiting to be filled, her color heightened. She marched up the stairs.

"I'm sorry, Nadine." He followed her. "It won't happen again."

"Damn right." She thought her voice would sound hoarse with misery, but it was iron-cold and passionless. She pulled out her clothes from the closet and flung them on the bed, dry-eyed and shivering.

"You're not leaving?"

She did not bother replying, but stuffed her rucksack with her meager belongings, leaving out everything she had bought in Florence or that Lawrence had give her. But she forgot to take the coral necklace from around her throat.

"Nadine." He came near her but did not touch her when he saw her warning expression. "I'll never do anything like that again. Tomorrow—we'll have Christmas your way. Just the two of us."

She swung the rucksack over her shoulder and headed past him to the door. Rage and grief battled for supremacy in her breast.

"I'm sorry," he repeated. "I didn't realize it would hurt you this much." He blocked the doorway and held out his hands. His bleak expression temporarily caused grief to gain the upper hand in the war, as she stared into his eyes. But rage was not beaten down.

"I'll never forgive you," she said, and she walked past him.

They went downstairs. Smoke issued from the kitchen area, and she almost wished the villa would catch fire and burn to the ground. She picked up Lawrence's car keys and headed for the front door.

"What's going on?" Lawrence shouted, and strode over to the kitchen. In response she slammed the front door behind her, just as he had done on countless occasions.

The night was cold, frosty. Her breath hovered like thin mist in front of her numb face. She got in the car and started the engine, not caring how Lawrence would get the car back to his house from the train station.

The other side door opened and he climbed in next to her.

"It's two o'clock on Christmas morning," he protested reasonably. "For God's sake, let's talk this over. There won't be any trains leaving for Rome tonight. We'll make a flight reservation and do this like adults."

"I've given you every chance to talk this over," she replied stiffly. "You've left it too late." The car rolled down the hill, and she set it into gear.

She would never forget that long drive through the black Christmas night, the stars sending needle-sharp shafts of light onto the dark road, the cold in the little car, Lawrence's hunched, brooding, angry expression. Twice she thought it had begun to rain and instinctively turned on the windshield wipers. They scraped across the dry windshield with an alarming screech, and she turned them off again and hastily brushed her eyes with the back of her hand instead. She drove up to the station entrance, switched off the engine, grabbed her rucksack, and marched up to the single open ticket vendor, not bothering to see if Lawrence would follow or whether he had come along simply to take his car back to the villa.

He was at her side in a flash.

"Not until six in the morning. I'm sorry," The tired-looking man informed Nadine.

Dully, she found a gray plastic chair to sit on in the smoky waiting room. Lawrence sat down beside her. She wondered if his car had been towed away yet; she hoped it had.

"You can't leave like this," she heard him saying. "After all we've meant to each other—"

She clenched her fists tightly. "You left me like this every single time we had an argument. No explanation, no apology; just slam the door and you're gone. Now it's my turn."

"But I came back."

"There's the difference."

She gripped her stomach, fighting a growing nausea. How

could she leave him like this? He was more important to her than the air she breathed. She could not live without him. It was impossible to go through with it.

"Please go, Lawrence," she heard herself saying. She was enveloped in a wave of sick darkness, hugging her contracting stomach. Her eyes were closed. "I can't bear it if you stay."

"Come with me."

"No." She was going to throw up. She fought the sickening tide and rose unsteadily. "Where's the bathroom?" she whispered.

He took her to one, supporting her, frightened for her. She remained inside for a long time, and emerging just when he was on the point of asking someone to check up on her.

"You don't feel well," he stated. "What's the matter with you?"

She kept hugging her stomach and trembling. "Please go. I can't stand being here with you for three more hours."

"I'm not going till you're on that train or in my car."

"Please, Lawrence."

They headed back to the hard, gray seats.

"Were you sick?" He was still worried.

"Yes," she cried, sitting down and burying her face in her hands. "You make me sick! Go away and leave me alone."

But for three grim hours Lawrence sat at her side, not talking. He bought cigarettes and smoked. Nadine let her hands fall from her ravaged face to wind around her belly again. It was true, she felt sick. Sick with love. "Never again," she whispered to herself more than once.

Train arrivals spewed passengers through the gate to fall rejoicing into welcoming arms. Departures were sparse. The sky paled. Purple shadows under Lawrence's eyes and on his unshaven cheeks made him seem gaunt and grim. When her train was announced, he finally spoke.

"We can't end it like this. Nadine, we just can't! Look at me. Just for a moment."

But she couldn't look at him. Something swelled in her chest, pressing against it with a pain that squeezed the air from her lungs and the love from the remains of her heart. She stumbled to the train. He caught her before she climbed up the metal steps to the door, wrapping his arms around her. Her entire body shuddered convulsively with the sobs that racked her.

Again the train departure was announced. She pulled away from his chest and rasped the back of her hand against her drowning eyes, willing the tears back into her aching throat. Then she looked up to meet his eyes in the last goodbye. As she did so she stepped away, backward, to the train.

Lawrence was looking at her, but he did not see her. In the brief moment that her vision cleared, Nadine stared, horrified, at his full eyes. Feeling her escape from his hold, he turned blindly away and felt his way toward the station entrance and the waiting car outside.

Nadine stared after him, still backing in slow motion. Then her own eyes burned with fresh pain and she pulled herself up the stairs onto the train.

Chapter Four

❧

"*Buona sera, signorina*. You have a visitor downstairs. A Signor Stebbing."

"Thank you. I'll be right down."

Nadine's clear gray eyes looked with reluctance and apprehension at her reflection in the full-length mirror behind the door. He's just a man I used to know, she told herself firmly. He's not the only man I ever loved; he's not the father of my son. He's rich, famous, gifted, and married, and I'm seeing him on *business*. Why feel nervous?

Her grave oval face looked paler than usual, the lips unsmiling. Her hands were clasped in front of her chest, as though trying to quiet the agitated reverberations inside. She wore a silver-gray silk blouse, unbuttoned at her throat, with elbow-length sleeves exposing her elegant wrists and slender hands. A white linen skirt hugged her slim waist and fell straight to her knees. Her legs were bare except for the flat Italian sandals on her feet. All she needed now, she thought ruefully, was the string of dark red coral that Lawrence had bought her four years ago. It would have added a much-needed splash of color to the subdued outfit. But she had purposely not brought that necklace with her. Instead she nervously fingered a string of moonstones, trying to order herself to go downstairs.

Her brown hair, parted on one side, fell in a wave down

the side of her face, half covering one of her apprehensive eyes. She pushed it back, debated tying it in a pony tail. No, she was simply stalling, she told herself crossly. Go downstairs and act as though you've never met. You can do it.

The gray eyes gazed back gravely, as though in doubt of her acting ability. Impatiently she broke away from her reflection and picked up her beige leather purse. Lawrence Stebbing was just an old friend with whom she had to discuss the business of the exhibition. As long as she remembered that, she would carry off the meeting without anguish.

The bedroom closed behind her with a decided click. She pushed her shoulders back, lifted her chin, and walked toward the elevator, her sandals making no sound on the plush hall carpet. Inside the wood-paneled elevator she rigidly steeled herself for the encounter.

The doors slid open and she stepped into the marble lobby. Her eyes scanned the crowd milling in the waiting room a few steps down from the reception area, searching for him. For a wild moment she wondered if she might fail to recognize him. It had been four years, after all. Could that large, burly-looking man be—

No. When her eyes finally lighted on him she knew him unmistakably. He stood with his back to her, his arms folded, looking out the window onto the street at the Arno River beyond. What was it about someone you knew that made them recognizable from their mere outline and form? Was it the broad shoulders in the well-fitting white shirt, slightly hunched in the determined manner that you remembered so well? Or the slender hips and long legs outlined by the casual gray corduroy pants that made him so familiar? No, other men had similar builds, Nadine thought, realizing her heartbeat was skipping rapidly. Yet she would recognize Lawrence in a crowd of a thousand and over a mile away. It was his own unique aura that had filtered its way through the crowded lobby to where she stood.

Almost as though he felt her studying him, Lawrence

turned toward her. Their eyes locked immediately; neither moved. For a long moment Nadine stood transfixed by the penetrating, brooding expression she knew well, then her knees began to shake. Literally to shake, she realized with irritation. What happened to the earlier admonishments to herself? Lawrence was just an old friend, a married one at that. Taking a breath, she walked unsteadily toward him.

As though drawn by a magnet, Lawrence came toward her at the same moment. They stopped when they were two feet apart. The air was charged with electricity; Nadine could almost feel the downy golden hair rise on the backs of her arms and on her bare legs. He was only an old friend; she was here on business—"

"Hello, Lawrence."

Bravely she held out her hand. It looked pathetically small and white, she thought, lost in Lawrence's powerful grip. For a moment she had a wild fear that his hand had imprisoned hers, like a wild creature captured by a ruthlessly indifferent stranger. She struggled frantically to regain possession of it and Lawrence released it, frowning. Her panic subsided, but her hand ached from the contact.

She offered him an apologetic smile.

"Hello, Nadine," he said.

Now that he was nearer to her she saw that he *had* changed. It wasn't just the deepened creases between his eyes or the new indented lines running down his gaunt cheeks to his strong jaw, but a feeling he gave her of weight and darkness. His forest-green eyes were warm, though, and a little uncertain.

It was the hint of uncertainty that gave Nadine the strength to speak. "Let's go. It's getting more crowded by the minute in here, isn't it? Some kind of convention, I suppose."

She led the way to the glass revolving doors, unable to decide whether she was relieved or irritated to discover Lawrence had lost none of his rugged attractiveness. She quelled the feeling, however: His attractiveness was his wife's business, not hers.

"I'm parked over here," he informed her, heading across the narrow street to the familiar white Fiat parked on the other side.

"It's still running?" Her voice *sounded* normal, didn't it?

"Yup."

The doors were unlocked, and they got in. Even the smell of the car was one she remembered distinctly, although she had not thought of it until that moment. It was a combination of old plastic, damp oil, and the after-shave Lawrence always used. She had not noticed this last in the lobby, but now, seated beside him, it wafted to her, sending a fresh, stinging memory of the fervent love they had once shared.

She glanced at him, irritated with her traitorous senses that threatened to stir her too deeply. His eyes met hers, and he held the ignition key in his hand instead of starting the engine.

"There's a lot to talk about," he began quietly.

From his expression she knew he was not referring to his exhibition. She clasped the purse in her lap, staring at it in confusion.

"No, please," she said, her voice sounding so cold she hardly recognized it. "As I said on the phone, it's sheer coincidence that we used to . . . know each other. Let's keep our conversation to your show."

A fleeting expression of irritation and pain crossed his face. His voice matched hers in coldness.

"As you please." The words were stiff.

They set off. Nadine stared out the little window, racked with indecision. He was right, of course. How could they plunge directly into business matters while their last, bitter parting still scraped to rawness every other memory they had? The thought of that interminable Christmas night still brought the taste of sickness to her mouth. Lawrence had tried to apologize by writing; now it was her turn. She swallowed.

"I will say one thing, though," she said hastily. "I wrote an awful letter in reply to yours. I'm sorry. In spite of what I said, I was grateful for your letter. It did help, although I didn't acknowledge that then.''

"You certainly didn't," he replied curtly.

Well, she had made the apology. If he chose not to accept it, there was nothing she could do. Discouraged, she fell silent again. She couldn't help worrying about Lily. It was inevitable that they meet, since she and Lawrence would have to look through the paintings in his studio at some point, but the thought filled her with dread. She remembered her as someone so bewitching, strong, and beautiful, with a power to match Lawrence's own. She had won a commitment from him, after all. Would Lily act confidently friendly toward her, as she had when she had been drunk on Christmas Eve? She could afford to be magnanimous, especially now, Nadine thought, praying that she herself would be able to match the confidence and friendliness she expected to find in Lawrence's wife. It was too late to feel bitter.

She stared out at the golden, grassy hills that rolled past them in gentle undulations under the fairy-tale blue of the evening sky. The man sitting beside her was a cheat, a liar, a selfish, unfaithful womanizer, and he was married, too. She dared not forget that: although she would make every effort to pretend she no longer harbored any resentment against him, or Lily.

The car drew up on the narrow, hedge-lined road that ran past Lawrence's villa. He switched off the engine and got out of the car. With a careful mask of cordiality she followed him down the familiar rose-bordered path to the oak door. She did not look around her, and if Lawrence noticed her apparent lack of interest in the familiar surroundings, he said nothing to let her know that he had. He pushed open the door and held it open. Nadine stepped inside.

Had she expected that Lily's presence in the house might have affected some changes there, added some sign of domesticity, of femininity perhaps? Certainly she had not expected to find the spacious living room exactly the same as it had been when she last saw it. The shiny, brick-red tiles stretched away from her to the patio at the back of the house; the simple sparse wood furniture was the same; the few paintings on the wall had not been replaced by ones more recent.

"Drink?" Lawrence offered as she set her purse on the low chair nearest the door.

"I'd love one."

"Scotch? Wine? Beer?"

"Scotch, with ice."

He turned to the kitchen area, and Nadine wandered slowly toward the patio. The evening sun had set, tinting the clear sky with a faded violet that melted into a pale yellow on the horizon. The field stretched away before her, a light mist gathering over it. A faint breeze sent ripples of the familiar sound of the rustle of tall grass to her sensitive ears. All her senses had been heightened that evening, making her taut with the strain of too much experience. She felt like a wild animal constantly alert for a sign of danger. The scent of late summer—a combination of dying wild flowers, dried grass, and a barely perceptible promise of chill—filled her lungs as she sighed.

For a moment she thought she could not bear it, she could not bear to sit through dinner in this beautiful place she had once called her home, talking to the man she had once lost her heart to, trying to be civil to the woman he had chosen to marry. She swallowed past an aching throat, determined to carry on with the business at hand. He would not know, *she could not let him know* . . .

"Here you are." Lawrence handed her a glass. "Have a seat."

"Thanks," she replied automatically, sitting down on the low, comfortable chair nearest her. "Is your . . . is Lily around?"

Lawrence took a seat opposite her and stretched out his

long legs in front of him, swirling the ice around in the glass
he held in his lap and eyeing it inquiringly.

"Lily?"

"Yes."

"The divorce was final over two years ago, Nadine," he
said abruptly. "What made you think I was still married?"

Confusion suffused her pale face with crimson, and shock
made her hesitate before answering. "In New York we never
heard otherwise, I suppose." She changed the subject quickly.
"Do you go back there ever?" Staring into her own glass she
wondered if he would have looked her up had he been in New
York.

"No," he said. "Tell me how it's doing."

"The same. Nothing changes." And as soon as the words
were off her tongue she realized their implication. She did not
want him to think her feelings for him had not changed. They
had, irreversibly.

She stood up abruptly and went down the three stone steps
to the gravel path running alongside the grassy field. The
information that Lawrence was divorced was creating havoc
in her breast, and she needed a moment to sort it out and
calm down. She sat on the bottom step, her back to him, her
arms wrapped around her knees. Why should the news that
Lawrence was unmarried affect her like this? Married or not,
he was still an egotistical, callous brute.

He stood beside her, not looking like a brute at all. His
words were understanding, without being condescending.

"It must be strange to be back."

"Yes, it is." She tried to make her tone light.

"Why don't I fix something for us to eat? I'm starving.
That'll give you a chance to be by yourself for a moment if
you'd like. If you don't like, come into the kitchen and
entertain me." He gave her his familiar crooked smile when
she glanced up, startled again, this time by his sympathy. She
had almost forgotten that side of him. He disappeared.
Brooding, Nadine stared out across the misty field.

If only he weren't so damned attractive, she thought. If only he weren't so damned nice, too. Lawrence had an abundance of charm when he chose. But when he didn't choose, he was cruel, selfish. She couldn't forget that side of him, either.

She stood up and went back into the house. If she stayed out there he would think their encounter was upsetting her.

"Can I help you?"

"Just sit down over there and talk to me. Tell me about the new galleries in New York. Any interesting ones?"

While he cooked a delicious-smelling fish and made a colorful salad, Nadine chattered inconsequentially about the New York art scene, which Lawrence had deserted several years earlier. On occasion he interjected questions about her own life there. Where did she live? Had she done any more work on her master's thesis? Did she have friends? Each time he became in the slightest bit personal, Nadine turned the conversation ruthlessly back to impersonal topics. He had no right to pry into her life now. Besides, she was terrified that something she said might reveal Jamie's existence.

They took plates, forks, and the food onto the patio, where Lawrence lit a candle and opened a bottle of red wine. The hills in the distance had turned deep purple, and the mist hovering over the fields was a lighter shade of mauve. It was lovely, Nadine thought, biting into the delicately flavored fish. And it wasn't just the fact that she was in Fiesole again that was so lovely; it was being with Lawrence.

He was in a good mood. He talked lightly, charmingly, ferreting out the topics of conversation that Nadine felt comfortable with and staying with those, paying her compliments, and making it clear that he cared about her still, even though the caring was that of a friend. Nadine could not help but be touched, and by the end of this meal she was relaxed enough to slip out of her sandals and loll back against the comfortable chair, her hands clasping the wineglass. She turned the conversation to the Mills Gallery again.

"Everett Mills told me you two had met. He saw a show of yours in Florence last year. What did you think of him?"

"To tell you the truth, I don't remember him very well. I do remember that he came to my studio for a brief visit. But we didn't talk much. He said he'd be in touch about exhibiting my stuff."

"He knew that we had met," Nadine informed him. "Did you tell him?"

"I had no idea you were in the remotest way connected to him then," he assured her, surprised. "I'm sure I didn't mention you."

"I wonder how he knew, then. He's very crafty about finding out information like that."

Lawrence looked at her sharply. "Is he a hard person to work for?"

She flushed. It was not very professional of her to discuss her boss with the artist whose work they were planning to exhibit.

"Oh, no! I meant smart. That's a better word." Lawrence looked unconvinced, and she went on hurriedly, "He told me about a painting you'd done that he very definitely wanted included in the show. He said it was your finest work, and that you thought so too. I hope you'll let me see it."

A wariness crept over Lawrence's face.

"What was it called?"

"*Tuscan Dawn*. You haven't sold it, have you? Everett was very emphatic that we include it."

His voice was strained. "No, I haven't sold it."

"May I see it?" She was mystified by his tone.

After a brief silence Lawrence stood up.

"If you like."

He did not switch on the light in the stairwell. Silver-blue twilight filtered in from the large windows onto the gleaming wooden stairs and whitewashed walls. They went through the large bedroom on the second floor to the studio on the third floor. Lawrence turned on a table lamp that flooded the room with a dim, yellow glow. Nadine looked around curiously.

It was the same studio, the easel in the same place under the large skylight, and the finished canvases still lining the walls. Lawrence methodically went through a row of paintings leaning against the far wall, while Nadine examined the paintings nearest her. One was a portrait of an elderly peasant woman struck by orange light from a setting sun. Lawrence had managed to create a mood of the passing of the day, and the passing of life, without losing any of the vibrancy and aliveness of the old woman. It was a wonderful painting, of course, but there was a new element which had crept into his more recent work that she had missed in his paintings of four years ago. She narrowed her eyes, trying to define what it was. She couldn't.

"Ah." Lawrence had found the painting, and Nadine looked up expectantly. He brought it toward her, but didn't turn it around until it was directly in the soft light. He seemed preoccupied, disturbed.

Nadine gasped. She was staring directly at herself. Naked, lying on Lawrence's low, wide bed, a stream of clear Italian sunshine falling on her breasts and stomach, a white sheet half wrapped around her bare legs, and her eyes gazing out of the canvas with an unmistakable expression of languid, sensuous, satiated desire.

For a long moment there was thick, bewildering silence. Nadine was unable to drag her eyes away from the canvas. Then the room was filled with sobbing. It took her a moment to realize the rasping sounds were emitted by herself. Lawrence set down the painting and strode to her.

"Nadine."

She backed away, burying her face in her hands, using the windowsill for support. How terribly deep her love for him had been! She did not think of the times he had left her, betrayed her; all she remembered was the times when he touched her body with thrilling caresses, his low, tender voice murmuring endearments to her, the hours and hours of talking and loving and simply being together. For a time she lost all sense of her whereabouts, retreating into her grief at the loss of their love.

Slowly, almost instinctively, she realized that he had left her alone in the studio, and she wondered if her unexpected reaction to his painting had irritated him. But still she could not repress the sobs that racked her slim body. He had given her Jamie, then left her to struggle alone with the painful birth and lonely survival. He had been responsible for the rift between her and her parents. He had married another woman, after telling her he wanted no commitments.

And he had broken her heart.

Seeing the trusting, adoring look on the girl's face in the painting reminded her with biting cruelty of how she had lost her heart to him. The tension that had been building since last week and the emotions she had fought to suppress flooded the gates of her iron will with the rushing force of that memory. The dam had collapsed.

Through a blur she saw Lawrence heading toward her again. He pressed a glass into her hand, refusing to allow her to recoil from him. A burning taste of brandy ripped through her. Lawrence held her, soothed her.

"It's all right. Everything's all right."

"I have to leave. Please. Let me go."

But he didn't let her go. He stroked her soft hair, and gently massaged the nape of her slender neck until her sobs quieted. At last her violent trembling ceased and she became aware of his strong arms supporting her, one hand buried in her thick hair and the other rhythmically circling her rigid back. Their bodies were pressed together, and what at first had been comforting, now became another sensation, one of trembling fire in her unsteady pulse.

His long, tapered forefinger lited her lowered chin so that her red-rimmed almond eyes were forced to meet his tender ones.

"Nadine. So beautiful—"

His lips brushed hers, gingerly, as though he was afraid she might leap out of his arms if he frightened her now. But her hands gripped his elbows and she gave a faint groan. A flame overtook the tender look in Lawrence's dark eyes. He placed his hands on either side of her face and brought his mouth to hers again.

Their tongues met, apprehensively at first, exploring familiar territory with a childlike anxiety that something might have been changed during their separation. But the only change was the taste of that first kiss: It was salt with tears.

Nadine's hands moved up from Lawrence's elbows to his shoulders, then wrapped around his neck, pulling him closer. The sweetness of his mouth evaporated the bitterness; the throbbing surge of excitement flooded the aching loneliness from her bones. She wanted him, in spite of everything. She still wanted him, even after all this time.

His voice was hoarse. "Sweetheart . . . how I've missed you."

His shirt was unbuttoned, and her hot cheek pressed against the broad, tanned chest. She heard his heart thumping loudly and rapidly inside. Her hands strayed to his belt. He groaned and found her willing mouth again. While his tongue penetrated deeply into it, his hands unbuttoned the silk blouse and slipped it off her shoulders so that she was standing only in her wispy white bra and the white skirt.

As though they were one, they found the short way to the low couch, and Lawrence laid her down. He knelt beside her on the floor, unzipped her skirt, and slipped it off, his eyes devouring her curving hips, her smooth legs. Nadine closed her eyes and felt him divest her of her filmy undergarments. His hand roamed up her legs, whispering endearments as he did so.

"Darling, I've missed you so terribly . . ," His voice was hoarse.

She did not think about what was happening. It had been

four years since she had felt his touch, and she was thirsty for it. Her slender arms wrapped around him.

"Baby, look at me," he pleaded, kissing her eyelids.

But she couldn't.

"You're the loveliest woman in the world," he said huskily, lowering himself on top of her. She gripped his tanned shoulders.

"It's been so long!" she gasped. "I need you—"

"I know, sweetheart. I know."

Their rhythmic passion began in earnest. Nadine's fingernails dug into his back. What power did this man have to affect her body like this? she wondered briefly, before she was swept away to the tremulous, heavenly edge of ecstasy.

"Please—"

"Sweetheart—"

They erupted together in a long, shuddering crescendo. She clung to him; he cried her name out loud.

Breathing heavily, Nadine opened her eyes and found herself gazing at Lawrence's cheek. His eyes were closed, but his hand caressed her hair with such tenderness she was afraid once more she might weep.

His eyes flickered open. They lay still, without talking, regarding each other for a long moment. Finally he rolled off her.

"We've put this off for too long," he said soberly, pulling her to a sitting position so that she rested her head on his shoulder.

She replied quietly, "Don't say that. Tonight we—I lost control, that's all. It wasn't serious."

His body stiffened, and she realized the sacred moment of communion had disintegrated with her words.

"We could argue that point," he replied. She heard his effort to control the emotion in his voice. "But I'm not in the mood. Let's go downstairs, okay? We didn't finish the wine. And there's still a lot of talking to do."

She nodded, sorry she had lost the passionate man of a few

minutes ago, but feeling more able to cope with an aloof Lawrence than a tender one. He picked up her bra from the floor and slipped it around her; hooking it up in back, then handed her the white panties. Watching him move, Nadine was awed by his still-muscular arms, the long thighs, the tanned, broad back with the rippling vertebrae and muscles. She used to love watching him walk around naked, she remembered, turning her attention to the buttons on her blouse. It was curious how little his body had changed in four years. She wondered if he had found her changed. Had he noticed a roundness in her belly, a mature softness to her breasts?

Downstairs, Lawrence filled both their glasses and they returned to the patio. The balmy night air hung around them, laden with the scent of damp grass and pine trees. The late-summer stars seemed heavy and dim.

"Tell me what happened when you left," Lawrence asked, pulling his chair closed to hers, not touching her.

"I went back to New York. You know that."

"Yes, but I want to know what really happened. Did you have a hard time finding a job? What was it like? Was it good seeing your parents again? Did you fall in love?"

She gave a half-smile.

"I'll answer in order. Yes, I did have a hard time finding a job, but I found one." Hard indeed, considering she was pregnant at the time. "It was okay." She hesitated. "Yes, it was good seeing my parents again." That wasn't a total lie, she reasoned. When she had first returned they had been jubilant. It was only when they learned about Jamie that they had refused to see her again. "And no, I'm not in love."

A shadow crossed his face. She noted it in some surprise. He could not be so egotistical as to imagine that she would still care for him after the hurt he inflicted on her and after the years separation! Besides, he was the one who had not been in love; he was the one who had left her for Lily. It was absurd to think he might be pained by her assertion.

She dropped her eyes to her glass, unable to look at him.

She might be frightened of him in some strange way, but she certainly did not love him. Feeling unreasonably angry, she stood up and refilled her glass with the ruby-red wine, then went to stand by the patio wall, her back to Lawrence, staring out at the mist hovering by the edge of the fields and the clear, indigo sky overhead. Far away a dog barked, the sound sending a stab of loneliness through her. A sudden yearning for Jamie enveloped her like a dark, heavy coat that she tried inwardly to wriggle out of.

"Nadine."

"Yes?" She did not turn around.

"I've done all the questioning. Aren't you going to ask me anything?"

She swallowed.

"There's nothing I want to know."

The dog barked again, and the sound unnerved her. Still she could not turn around, for if she did he would surely see the poignant yearning for her son that burned her eyes. Could he tell—was there a way he could know about Jamie? Didn't he feel a small part of himself sharing the universe; could he not instinctively sense the bond tying him to the unknown child he had fathered? Nadine felt so transparent she wondered if he could see right through her.

His voice reached her again, bringing her back from the night-filled, lonely fields and too-big sky that filled her soul with unexplainable sadness, back from the insistent tug on her heartstrings for Jamie thousands of miles away, back from the swift memories of four years ago that kept overtaking her, without warning, and without respite.

"There's something *I* want *you* to know," he said.

Lily. He was going to talk about Lily. She turned abruptly.

"Please." Her voice was hoarse. "Don't tell me."

He was sitting on the low chair, long legs stretched out, dark eyes fastened on hers, speculatively, like Jamie's when he was about to tell her something but wanted to be sure he had her complete attention. But she refused to give it to

Lawrence. She stared down at the glass in her hand, not seeing it.

Lawrence joined her by the low stone wall, bringing with him a comforting human strength that helped drive away the mystery and awe of the world beyond the patio. Without moving her head she could focus her gaze on his tanned, powerful hands holding the wineglass in front of the black leather belt with the simple brass buckle. The soft gray corduroys were blurred in the outer rim of her vision.

"We have to talk about it," he said quietly. "You have to know why I married Lily when all you heard from me when we lived together was that I didn't want any kind of commitment in a relationship." Nadine's eyes lifted to his at last, listening. Was this particular thorn about to be pressed still more deeply into her breast by his words, or would it be miraculously, blessedly, removed? He continued: "Lily told me she was pregnant. She's an Italian, you know, and her family are Catholic. She couldn't have an abortion and she couldn't have the child illegitimately without utter degradation and ostracism from the only society she knew. Her only recourse was for me to marry her. It was a hard decision for me to make, because I valued my independence and freedom as much as my honor and sense of duty. Honor and duty won over." He drew a breath. "You know why it won over, Nadine? Because of you. Your talk about responsibility and commitment had struck home, somewhere, and kept reemerging at the oddest times. I had lost you, but I had learned from you. So I married Lily."

"Please," Nadine protested brokenly. "I don't want to hear about your damned motives for marrying Lily. I don't care. I simply don't care."

Lawrence stared at her bowed head with puzzled anger, then turned away to go into the house. The thorn had not been removed, and it did not pierce her more deeply than it had before, she thought. Nothing had changed. But Jamie had a half brother, or sister, somewhere on the planet. She felt sadder, if possible, at this new revelation, realizing that it meant Lawrence would probably be indifferent to Jamie's existence, since he already had a legal child. Shouldn't she be relieved? Instead she was devastated. The stars were motionless, unblinking. The velvet sky wrapped her in folds of incomprehensible strangeness, making her feel completely alone in the universe. Then a faint stab pierced her again. Not alone—there was Jamie. But so far away!

She heard Lawrence return to the patio and turned to him with relief. Even hearing about Lily was better than being alone out here.

She gave him an apologetic smile, and they both spoke at once:

"I'm sorry—"

"I'm sorry—"

Then they laughed nervously.

"Want some brandy?" he offered, setting two snifters on the low table and uncorking the bottle.

She glanced at her watch, and seeing the gesture, he threw her a crooked smile.

"I won't talk about anything you don't want to hear," he promised. "Don't go yet. It's not even midnight."

Acquiescing with a laugh, she returned to her chair and told him, "Midnight! I'm usually in bed by ten in New York. I forgot how late you stay up."

She took a sip of the brandy he handed her. When he had first brought her here, during that electric, torrential storm, he had given her brandy to warm her up. Now she needed it again, for a different kind of warming. Had he guessed how empty and cold she felt inside?

She felt a warmth spreading through her tense body, evaporating the bewildering sorrow of a few minutes ago.

"Do you like going to bed early?" he asked.

She replied honestly, "There's no reason not to. And I have to wake up at six-thirty—"

"Six-thirty!" he broke in laughing. "That's crazy! I could never get you out of bed before midday."

"I know," she remembered. But then, in those days they usually stayed up till dawn, making love and talking and making love again.

"Why so early? You don't have to be at the gallery till ten or so, do you?"

"No, but . . ." she floundered, realizing that she had almost given away the fact that she had to have Jamie at school by twenty past eight. "There's lots to do in the mornings," she finished lamely, avoiding his interested gaze. She cupped the glass with both hands and stared into the amber liquid with an effort.

"Do you live by yourself?" he asked next.

Her eyes flew to his, startled, alarmed.

"What do you mean?"

He was curious. "Do you have a roommate?"

"No." Her son couldn't be counted as a roommate, exactly.

"A boyfriend?"

"No."

He frowned. "Why not?"

"Does that surprise you?" she said with a small laugh.

"Very much. You're a born giver, Nadine, and I can't imagine you with no one around to be a receiver and a reciprocator."

It was foolish to be touched by the casual words, she thought, but she was. She took another sip of brandy.

"I 'give' at my job, and to my friends," she replied slowly. "I'm not really interested in having a relationship with someone at the moment."

"Too busy?"

"That's not the real reason." She sought around for an explanation. "It's more that I don't want to get involved in a . . ." She hesitated. "In a casual affair again, I'd want total commitment. I need the security."

"How you've changed," he remarked drily.

"Yes," she said simply. "Although maybe I haven't really changed—maybe I always was like this and just didn't realize it when I was with you. You were so eloquent in your arguments for free love that you had me persuaded for a while. But it was only a matter of time before I realized that I didn't really believe in a noncommitting relationship for myself."

His eyebrows were drawn, interestedly, alertly. "But what if you fell in love again? Would love give you 'security'?"

"Oh, no." Again her eyes flew to his, then dropped to the glass again. "Quite the opposite, judging from experience." Her lips trembled in a half-smile.

"You're saying if someone offered to marry you and you didn't love him, you'd still marry him?"

"If I cared for him enough."

"And if you loved someone, but he didn't want to marry you, you wouldn't agree to have an affair?"

She nodded. "That's why tonight was a—" she began hesitantly.

"Yes, I see," he interrupted. Then he gentled his voice unexpectedly. "Well, we all learn from our mistakes, don't we? My marriage to Lily was so disastrous and the divorce so wretched that I've sworn off marriage forever. I've realized my first instincts were the right ones. Free love and passionate affairs are a hell of a lot more rewarding."

Strangely enough his words made her laugh. It was as though they had both sworn off each other by the goals they had set for themselves and by doing so had placed their relationship on a new footing: one of understanding friendship.

"Perfect," she said, smiling at him. "We're both safe from each other."

He gave an affectionate growl and finished his brandy in a gulp. Feeling light-headed, Nadine poured them both more. She knew she should leave, but she didn't want to. Not yet.

"Where is—your child?" she asked, curling her legs under her on the chair.

He looked up sharply.

"What?"

She was taken aback by his exclamation.

"You said you married Lily because she was pregnant."

He relaxed. "Oh. You didn't let me finish. There was no child. Lily wasn't pregnant. She lied, in order to get me to marry her."

"Oh, no." Sympathy and dismay flooded Nadine's face. No wonder he was cynical about marriage!

He went on gruffly, "The whole sordid episode made me loathe the concept of marriage and the idea of a family too. It's funny, because when Lily first told me she was pregnant I got excited about being a father. But now I hate the idea."

Nadine froze. What a hideous thing to say, she thought furiously, thinking of her brave, fatherless son in New York. She set her glass down.

"I have to leave," she informed him coldly. She slipped her bare feet into the sandals. Lawrence started to protest but she cut him off. "It's very late for me. I'd like to go."

"Have I said something?"

"Nothing that you haven't said before." She stood up and headed inside the house. She had felt so many different things during the course of the emotionally charged evening that this final flood of anger for Jamie's sake was nothing more than another drop in the bucket of her emotions.

"Okay, I'm ready." Lawrence appeared beside her, car keys in hand. In silence he led the way along the narrow path to the street and got in the front seat of the car. Nadine climbed in next to him.

They drove to the hotel in complete silence. Lawrence was frowning, his dark eyes concentrated on the winding road ahead of them. Nadine stared stiffly out the window. Poor Jamie, she thought bitterly. What had he done to deserve a father with sentiments like Lawrence's?

The car pulled up in front of the hotel. Without a word

Nadine got out and slammed the car door as hard as she could before walking up the stairs to the revolving door.

Lawrence leaped out and grabbed her wrist before she reached the top stair. He swung her around, gripping her so tightly it hurt. The anger in his eyes matched hers.

"Why did you slam the door?" he asked furiously.

She tried to release her wrists, but he tightened his grip. He repeated:

"Why did you slam the door?"

"Let me go." Rage choked her.

"Answer me."

"Let me go."

Nadine struggled to break away from Lawrence's savage kiss. Her mouth was crushed to his, and she was locked in his powerful grasp. Damn him, she cried silently. Damn him, damn him, damn him. She hadn't cursed him like this in a long time, but she could not help responding to his brutal, relentless kiss.

He released her abruptly.

"I'll call you tomorrow." The anger had died in his eyes; now they were cold. "We have more business to discuss."

She could not reply. Couldn't he see how much she hated him? She whirled away and pushed the revolving door so hard that it spun around after she had disappeared into the lobby.

She slammed her bedroom door hard behind her, not caring about her neighbors. She tore off her clothes and stepped into the shower, wanting to cleanse herself of everything that had been tainted with Lawrence's touch. Yes, they would discuss business tomorrow, and only business! How she wished she could avoid seeing him again. Ever.

She accidentally gulped and was surprised to find the water tasted salty. When she turned off the shower tap and stepped onto the fluffy white bath mat she glimpsed herself in the steamy mirror and saw that she was crying again, without realizing it.

"I'm tired," she said, stumbling into the bedroom without drying herself properly. She hugged the towel around her chest. "I'm just so tired."

She collapsed onto the freshly made bed and buried her wet face and hair in the plump, fresh pillow.

Chapter Five

Nadine awoke the following morning with a slight hangover. Her blurry gaze traced the brown outlines of ragged-edged flowers on the coffee-colored wallpaper beside her head, then traveled to the beige carpet littered with the garments she had worn the previous evening. Her hair had not dried properly after her shower and the pillow was flat and damp.

Gingerly she sat up and pushed some strands of hair from her eyes, trying to recollect what had happened at Lawrence's villa. An agonizingly sweet memory of making love in the dimly lit studio made her close her heavy eyes briefly.

Then she got out of bed and padded over to the window. Sharp sunlight stabbed her eyes when she drew apart the shiny gold curtains, making her blink. The morning air was fresh, however, and she guessed it was not late. Below the tiny balcony the Arno sparkled gaily in the sunshine, as though someone had dropped thousands of diamonds on the shimmering ripples. If she craned her neck she could glimpse the Ponte Vecchio farther down the river. She sighed. How lovely Florence was!

The bedside telephone rang.

"Hello?"

"Hi, Nadine, Sleep well?" It was Lawrence, wide-awake, brusque, confident.

"Yes, thanks."

"Have you had breakfast?"

"Not yet." Where did he find his energy?

"Can I take you out? I'll pick you up in about half an hour."

They still had to discuss the business of his show, which had barely been touched on last night, Nadine remembered. The sooner that was taken care of the sooner she could return to Jamie.

"Okay."

"I'll meet you downstairs."

"Okay," she repeated, wishing she could coax her voice into a semblance of friendliness. It sounded so stuffy, so cold, not at all like hers. "See you then."

If Lawrence was going to act cordially toward her, then she would try to match his civility. Last night had been too tumultuous to relive, even in memory, especially their final quarrel. Nadine remembered what he had said to anger her: something about hating the thought of being a father. All her maternal instincts had flared up in revolt, thinking of Jamie. But now her rage seemed an absurd overreaction. It was ridiculous for her to want him to tell her that he longed to discover he had a son—somewhere. Besides, shouldn't she be relieved to know that Lawrence, were he to discover the fact of Jamie's existence, would not want custody of the child, since the thought of being a father was repugnant to him?

Naked, Nadine opened the closet. They would probably spend at least some of the day walking around Florence, as well as looking through Lawrence's canvases. She decided to wear a navy blue skirt and a cream-colored blouse. It was too warm for a sweater or jacket, so after slipping into her comfortable sandals and brushing her hair, she was ready to leave. She glanced in the mirror. Gray eyes, their almond shape more pronounced because of the headache she was fighting, gazed levelly back. What were you frightened of yesterday, old girl? she asked herself. That you'd fall in love with Lawrence all over again? Or that you'd hate him so much you wouldn't be able to stand him? But now you've discovered he's just a guy, a nice guy. He doesn't like kids; he doesn't want to get married—ever. You've got Jamie, and you want to be married so that you can devote yourself to Jamie while he's young. Therefore there's no reason the two of you can't have a pleasant day discussing business and seeing Florence without getting emotionally entangled again. Right?

Why did the gray eyes look disbelieving? Did they expect she would be just as affected by Lawrence as she had been yesterday? Nadine told herself crossly: "Even if he antagonizes you or tries to get too personal or intimate, there's no reason for you to fly off the handle. You've just got to keep a level head, remain civil, cheerful, and disinterested. After all, you don't want him to think he can affect you anymore. The time when he had power over your emotions is over."

Over. She repeated the word to herself when she shut the bedroom door behind her and walked down the hallway to the elevator. Lawrence had not yet arrived. She went down the three short steps to the waiting room, practically deserted at this hour, and sat down, composing her features into an expression of friendly indifference and determined to maintain it throughout the day.

"Good morning!" Lawrence looked as though he was going to kiss her cheek, but he was prevented by the hand she held out to him and her cool greeting.

"Good morning, Lawrence. Where are we going for breakfast? I'm starved."

He released her hand and kept his dark friendly eyes fastened on her as she stood up. Nadine led the way to the street.

Lawrence did not bring up last night's quarrel, but he did insist that business could wait and that Nadine should have a chance to see Florence once again. So instead of going to his villa after breakfast, they set off toward the Pitti Palace, where they made their first stop, then wandered over to the Uffizi. The strain of maintaining her easygoing, friendly demeanor was greater than she had anticipated. She was torn between lingering bitterness, searing nostalgia, and genuine enjoyment of Lawrence's company. Every reminder of their past relationship—a glimpse down a familiar street, a sculpture they had both adored, a quiet, empty church where they had once found shelter during a sudden cloudburst—each of these struck her afresh with a raw poignancy that persistently prodded the still-tender bruise in her heart. She kept up an admirable show of spirits, however, as they wandered the friendly little city, talking animatedly about everything that was not important. After several hours of walking and visiting museums they stopped at a restaurant for lunch. Nadine protested when Lawrence ordered a bottle of wine to accompany the fresh fish they'd ordered, but he overrode her objection.

"We don't have to finish it," he pointed out. "But it's one of the best wines I've found in the city, and I'd like you to try it."

Put like that, how could she refuse? And it did taste delicious: crisp, light, and flavorful. The afternoon sun bounced off the Arno bubbling past outside, sending flickering glances of light onto the cream-colored walls of the restaurant and reflecting off the heavy silverware and sparkling glasses on the tables. The thick white tablecloth became spattered with bread crumbs, spilled asparagus, fresh peas; the wine glasses were filled and refilled, their conversation was like the reflection of the sun on the river: darting, inquisitive, and blindingly bright.

They lingered over their espresso coffees, talking about Lawrence's show and the ideas Nadine had for it. Cigarette smoke wreathed languidly around ther heads from the other diners; at one point Nadine meant to ask Lawrence why he no longer smoked, but the question evaporated and she forgot it before she had the opportunity. Lazy and satisfied in the heavy afternoon atmosphere, they continued their discussion over a second round of espressos, leaning back in the wooden chairs, hardly aware of the fact that they were the sole remaining customers.

Can't he see, Nadine cried in her heart when they finally rose to leave, can't he see how difficult it is for me to keep up this pretense of friendliness? Doesn't he realize how hard this is for me? But Lawrence continued conversing pleasantly when they set off once more, as though they saw each other every day, as though she had not been away for years, as though they had never been parted. . . .

She matched his tone for the sake of her pride and her job, responding with cordial interest, refusing to express her anguish at having been separated from the man and the city she loved. It wasn't until late afternoon that the cloak of friendly reserve she had carefully wrapped around her fell slightly and she accidentally allowed him to see the depth of her suffering.

He had persuaded her to go to the top of the Campanile so that she could have a view of the city and the fairy-tale hills in the distance. Nadine knew she should not risk it, for she had recently developed a phobia about heights, but she was unwilling to explain to Lawrence that she suffered from vertigo and acquiesced in silence. She followed him into the elevator and clenched her fists tightly as the little car slowly climbed the bell tower.

Outside, however, the rush of loud voices and wind and the dizzying height made it hard to restrain hysterical screaming. She clung to the inside wall. Lawrence looked around in surprise when he saw that she did not follow him to the balcony rail. He returned to her side immediately.

"What's the matter?"

She was shaking. A howling darkness threatened to drown her. She imagined herself falling—falling into the blackness. She gripped onto something tightly, trying to save herself. Then she heard Lawrence's steady voice and realized she was desperately clinging to his hand.

"Nadine, what's wrong?"

Still she could not speak, afraid that if she opened her mouth a fearful scream would emerge. She dared not open her eyes. If she pretended she was on the ground, if she kept her eyes hidden from the perilous sweeping sight of the city far below, she would be all right.

The elevator reappeared, and Lawrence, his arm around her, led her back to the car. Dizzy with relief, Nadine leaned her head against his shoulder. Her knees still shook, but Lawrence's strong arm around her helped keep her upright. Still clinging to him, she left the tall, thin building. Lawrence sat her down on a stone bench in the little courtyard outside. She tried to stop her trembling, humiliated by the absurd fear that she could not control.

"Tell me what happened," Lawrence insisted quietly.

Now that the earth was firmly under her she felt able to reply. "Nothing serious. I—I get attacks of vertigo occasionally. I thought maybe I'd gotten over it, but it seems that I haven't yet."

"Vertigo!" he exclaimed in amazement. "You never used to be scared of heights! We went up the Campanile several times."

"I know. It started happening after I got back to New York."

There was a short silence. Lawrence's expression was of astonishment.

"What happened in New York that made you change so much?" he asked at last. "Won't you tell me?"

She threw him a nervous glance but answered softly, "Don't you think you might have changed me that much? You were cruel then—worse, indifferent. You must have imagined I'd be affected somewhat by your treatment of me." She could no longer hide the bitterness from her voice.

Standing in front of her, Lawrence replied quietly, "I was never indifferent to you."

"Indifferent enough to desert me." Her trembling was ebbing all the energy from her body.

"I never deserted you." Lawrence's voice was still quiet. "You've exaggerated what I did way out of proportion. I was honest with you from the start: I wanted my freedom and my independence, and I wanted you as well. You accepted me on those terms. You were the one who deserted me, when you changed your mind about our relationship. But I didn't hold your jealousy and possessiveness against you for four years. You'll have to drop your cherished illusion that you were a perfect companion and lover and I was a bastard."

Nadine buried her round pale chin in her small hands and stared down at the reassuring tufts of grass that poked out from between the cobblestones.

"Maybe," she said finally. "But it isn't really a question of wrong and right. You were older, more experienced, wiser in the ways of the world. You should have been able to see what I couldn't see. I was much too immature to understand what the hell you meant by freedom and independence. You should have known that I was bound to get homesick eventually, no matter how much I maligned my parents to you." She paused. "You should have understood when I got jealous, instead of just getting angry and contemptuous and walking off and making me even more jealous."

Lawrence stuck his hands in his pockets and watched her sandalled toe scrape back and forth against a shiny gray cobblestone, crushing several tender blades of grass into the cracks.

"I did expect too much from you," he admitted slowly. "Especially considering your age and background."

"And I expected too much from you," she couldn't help saying, "considering how insensitive and selfish you were."

He stiffened. "My only mistake was in doing what I said all along I would do."

Crushed by the argument, Nadine felt her throat ache. The man no longer had power over her emotions: Why then did she feel this bewildering grief at the thought of his contempt, at the thought of their upcoming separation, at the thought that Jamie would never get to know his father?

"And my only mistake was to fall in love with you." She tried to swallow. "And also in being too blind to see that you didn't love me, and would eventually get tired of me. It simply never occurred to me that one day you might actually not love me, not want me." She stood up abruptly. In an effort to counteract the agony he might perceive in her eyes she tried to smile. "That's probably why I got scared of heights: I fell in love and no one was there to catch me when I hit the bottom."

Lawrence did not reply. By mutual consent they began walking again, their earlier lightheartedness banished by the thoughtful, unhappy silence that settled between them. Although Nadine was sorry she had been unable to repress her bitterness, she was glad that Lawrence's complacency had been shattered. If he was going to spend his life hurting women, he'd better be aware of the damage he was doing.

"I didn't mean for our conversation to get so personal again," Nadine spoke at last. "We really should just stick to business."

"How can we not get personal after last night?" Lawrence asked, sounding exasperated and angry. "Didn't you feel anything when we made love?"

She kept on walking.

"Answer me," he insisted. "Didn't you feel anything?"

"That was a lapse; a combination of jet lag and an old habit. I'm not interested in having an affair with anyone, least of all you. I want security, financial support, commitment, loyalty—"

He interrupted her coldly, "You haven't answered my question."

Her eyes narrowed.

"No, Lawrence, I didn't feel anything when we made love. Certainly not enough to want to do it again." She injected a note of sarcastic kindness into her tone: "Don't worry, though, about not having anyone when you're in New York. I'm sure we can find someone for you. I'll put out an advertisement for you and you can screen the applicants when you arrive."

Lawrence's eyes blackened, and for a moment she feared she had gone too far, but he controlled his temper.

"I'll take you back to your hotel. We'll finish talking about the arrangements for the show in the morning."

"Good," she replied evenly. "I'm planning on making a reservation for my flight home tomorrow afternoon."

He did not answer, and they walked the rest of the way in silence. When he took his departure he said coolly, "See you tomorrow," turned on his heel, and returned to the parked car.

Nadine stared after him, then quickly headed for the elevator. More than ever she longed to be safe with Jamie in her drab little apartment, cooking, reading cozily, sleeping safely alone. The rhythm and tedium of the working week seemed like a haven from the emotional turmoil of the past two days. She opened her bedroom door and slammed it behind her, trying to slam out her conflicting emotions as well.

But guilt at her rudeness to Lawrence struck her when she was alone. She hugged her stomach tightly. There was such tenderness and compassion in Lawrence, such understanding and intelligence and humor, that she longed to forget the past, forget her heartache, and obey only the persistent longing to simply be with him. It wasn't true that she had felt nothing when they made love last night: She was afraid even now of what she had felt. The fiery passion which had faded into thick, stone-cold ashes in her chest had somewhere retained a lingering warmth which smoldered into glowing embers at the touch of his hand, the taste of his mouth. She had tried to crush the need she felt for his virile, fulfilling lovemaking, but in just a few hours of being with him her body had succumbed to its bittersweet desire. If she allowed it to, would her heart succumb as well? And by doing so would it destroy the independence in which she had found refuge? Would her heart forget, as her traitorous body had forgotten last night, the agony Lawrence had once caused her, and could cause again?

It would be sweet heaven to be able to forget, she thought, kicking off her sandals and stretching out on the soft bed. Forget, forget, forget. The words resounded in her brain. Forget the past; forget her love for Lawrence; forget her bitterness. If only she could do that, they could be friends. Funny, but she longed to be friends with Lawrence now. He had once meant more to her than anyone in the world. If they couldn't be lovers, she would still like to be able to replace that special place in her heart that she would always hold for him with friendship.

She rolled over onto her stomach and buried her face in the smooth pillow. How could they be friends? How was it possible to ignore her frenzied heartbeat when she saw him, his electric touch, the sparking currents that jumped erratically between them. Friends could not be so sensitive, so overly charged with emotion. Friends could not behave like the polar opposites of a magnet, irresistably pulled toward one another by the force of their physical attraction.

Willing herself to overcome her feeling of desolation, Nadine reached over and picked up the telephone to make her flight reservation for the following afternoon.

Chapter Six

"No, he hasn't changed much." Nadine sipped Perrier and avoided her curious sister's scrutiny. She had stopped drinking almost entirely since her return from Florence, having decided that her emotional instability was partly due to the effect of the alcohol.

"Did you meet his wife?"

"They were divorced two years ago." Although she had been expecting these questions, she found herself unwilling to describe her visit to Florence in detail. Charlotte was still as hostile toward Lawrence as ever, but Nadine's own feelings were not as simple as they had been a few weeks ago. He had made a good case for himself in reviewing the reason for their separation, although she had not admitted it to him at the time, and she was beginning to see that the blame lay not entirely at his door. She tried to suggest this to Charlotte, with little success.

"He cheated on you and left you with a child! He's entirely guilty!"

So Nadine changed the subject. She was worried about Jamie. He had grown increasingly difficult since she had been away, and now that the arrangements for Lawrence's show were taking up so much of her time, he was left too much to Charlotte's complacent care. He was often sullen and obstinate, and Nadine had received more than one telephone call from his kindergarten teacher, complaining of unruliness in class. Nadine longed for Lawrence's show to be over so that she could devote more time to Jamie and get him back on the affectionate, good-natured track she used to know. But he was resentful of the time she spent away from him, and did not forgive her quickly when they were finally together in the short evenings, although she tried to explain to him the reason for her neglect of him.

September passed in a turmoil of activity and difficulties. Pleased with the way the show was going, Everett paid unwelcome attention to Nadine and acted thoroughly annoyed when she continued to insist that she had to be home in the evening and could not go out with him. He had asked persistent, intimate questions about her stay in Florence when she had first returned, and only by responding with a firmness bordering on rudeness, did Nadine finally silence him.

"You sent me to Florence to handle some administrative details of the show. That's what I did. There's nothing else I have to report on." And containing herself with some difficulty, she left his office, closing the door sharply behind her.

Everett called Nadine into his office several days before Lawrence's arrival and gave her strict orders regarding his stay in New York. He wanted her to spend as much time as possible with Lawrence.

"As long as his paintings are in our gallery, Stebbing is our client. I want him treated with the respect all our clients deserve. That includes meeting him at the airport, escorting him to museums, galleries, plays—just be sure to tell me in advance which ones you'll be attending. And I want you to use your expense account for lunches, drinks, and dinners."

"But there are a hundred things that still have to be taken care of here at the gallery, and he's arriving on Thursday!" Nadine protested.

"Make a list of everything that needs to be done and Donna will take care of it." He lit a cigarette and blew a cloud of smoke into the room. Nadine regarded him uncertainly, wondering what he had up his sleeve. "Does Stebbing know of your son's existence?"

"No." Her voice was even. Did Everett know Jamie was Lawrence's child?

"I'll make a bargain with you, sweets. If you do exactly as I ask, Stebbing won't hear about his kid from me."

She whitened. So he did know!

"Don't look alarmed. My powers of deduction aren't so bad. *Tuscan Dawn* was painted several months before the date of your son's birth. I know from experience that you aren't promiscuous—it was only logical to assume Lawrence was your son's father." He inhaled again. "So he doesn't know yet, eh?"

Her gray eyes were angry and opaque. "I don't want him to know."

"I've told you he won't know unless you don't keep to your end of the bargain. You can trust me." He took a folder from his drawer. "Here's your itinerary. I want you to follow it."

She opened the folder. Inside was a detailed outline of press conferences, excursions, restaurants, and parties they were to attend, with reservation slips, passes, and formal invitations in a side pocket. Nadine tried to keep the despair from her voice.

"I can't leave my son alone this much. My job doesn't include working at night. I'll do everything else, but I have to spend the evenings with Jamie."

"Sorry, sweetie. You'll do everything on the list or Stebbing finds out about Jamie and you'll find you won't have any more evenings with Jamie ever again. You know what will happen if he finds out, of course. You wouldn't have a prayer of convincing a jury that you can properly care for a child on your own and with your salary."

Despite the warmth of the small office, Nadine shivered.

"You seem to have forgotten something." Her throat was dry.

"What's that?"

"Lawrence Stebbing himself. He won't want to go to half these things. What if he refuses?"

"I'm counting on you to make sure he doesn't refuse."

Nadine folded her arms, fighting a rising hysteria. "Why are you doing this?"

Everett's eyes were shuttered, blank.

"The only thing that concerns me is the success of my gallery, and that depends on this show. I have no hidden motive. I want the show to be a success, and with your cooperation it will be."

For a long moment they eyed each other warily, then Nadine left the office. Out in the corridor she shivered again, imagining the danger, the difficulties. If only she could read Lawrence's mind and know what he was thinking. What if the revelation that he was going to be spending twelve hours a day with her was repugnant to him? What if he wanted to prowl around for a woman he could spend the night with?—because she certainly was not going to be that woman! Not again!

She entered her office and shut the door. There was a way of getting out of this, of course. She could tell Lawrence about Jamie. But what if Lawrence changed his mind about being a father and decided he wanted Jamie with him in Florence? She could not put Jamie through a custody battle; she could not afford it anyway. No, Everett was right: Until she was absolutely certain she could trust Lawrence he could not know about Jamie.

A few days later Nadine woke feeling curiously elated, the way she used to feel on her birthday when she was a little girl. For a moment she wondered why her heart beat with such rapidity. Then she remembered. Lawrence was arriving today.

She tried her best to quell her excitement. It had been a month since she had seen him, and although they had talked several times on the telephone, their conversations had been brief and impersonal. Perhaps he'd realized how lucky he was to be free from her, she thought, remembering with a cringe how vindictive, immature, and bad-tempered her behavior had been.

Lawrence gave no sign that he was surprised to be met at Kennedy airport by Nadine. He pressed her hand firmly, holding it a moment too long, and her heart stepped up in gear. He wore a navy blue pinstripe suit, the jacket accentuating his broad shoulders and slim hips. A striped blue-and-green tie gave him a formal appearance. His dark brown hair was brushed to one side and had been recently trimmed. Even his hands made him seem formal, the dark-haired fingers and tanned skin jutting unfamiliarily out of the cuffs of his jacket. Remembering Everett's warning, Nadine smiled warmly and was surprised to feel herself illuminated briefly by the flashing lights of cameras.

"Welcome to New York, Mr. Stebbing." A man approached them, notebook in hand. "Are you glad to be back?"

Lawrence glanced at Nadine and frowned. She looked puzzled.

"Very glad," he replied shortly and tried to step past him.

Persistently the man barred his way. "Do you intend to stay here long?"

But Lawrence outmaneuvered him, keeping a firm grip on Nadine's arm, and strode toward the exit, his suitcase in his hand. The blinking camera flashes had made several people turn to stare at them. They waited impatiently in the taxi line. A large, heavily made-up woman appeared beside Nadine, seemingly out of nowhere. Enormous gold-hooped earrings bounced energetically as she spoke.

"Miss Barnet, is this your first reunion with Mr. Stebbing in four years?"

Furiously, Nadine willed the line to move forward.

"I don't see that it's your business," she said stiffly,

pointedly turning her back. They reached the front of the line and got into the yellow taxi quickly.

"The Pierre Hotel, please. Sixtieth and Fifth Avenue."

"Do those guys hang around the airport and photograph everyone who gets off the plane, hoping they might accidentally shoot someone famous?" Lawrence inquired lightly, turning to Nadine.

She made an equally light rejoinder, but a suspicion nagged her mind. Had Everett arranged for the press to be at the airport? Did he imagine Lawrence would take kindly to this sort of publicity, even for the sake of his show? Was that why he wanted her to be sure Lawrence was constantly in the limelight while he was in New York, to gain the public visibility that would ensure success with the press? Remembering Lawrence's publicity-shy anger with cameramen in Italy, Nadine devoutly hoped Everett had not done anything so stupid.

Manhattan jutted up into the blue haze across the East River. Sunlight bounced off the thousands of windows in a dazzling display. It was a beautiful fall day, cloudless, warm, breezy. Lawrence flashed her a smile.

"Looks just the same. Nothing changes, as you said in Florence."

She returned his smile and replied easily, temporarily putting aside the unexpected encounter with the press.

The driver let them off outside the cream-and-gold awning of the Pierre Hotel and the doorman ran to open the car door. Nadine paid for the ride, making sure she had a receipt for Everett, and followed Lawrence to the receptionist's desk. When he had registered they were shown up to his room overlooking Central Park. Nadine stared around, surprised by Everett's extravagance. It was large and luxurious, with a wide bed, television, a soft, silver carpet, two comfortable armchairs, and a balcony, which she did not go near.

"Does this look okay?" she asked.

He was surprised by her anxious tone. "Does your boss

think I'm going to cancel my show if I'm not pleased with the room I've been given?'' he asked. ''Don't worry. This is fine. Can I order you a drink?''

Nadine shook her head. ''I should leave you to unpack and settle in. Besides, I have to get back to the office and finish up some things.'' She backed uneasily to the door.

Lawrence took off his jacket and tossed it carelessly on the bed, then loosened his tie.

''How about dinner? I'd like to hear how things are going.''

She gave him an uncertain smile. ''I don't know if you're going to like this, Lawrence, but you're doomed to have dinner with me every night until your opening. Not just dinner, either.''

Lawrence's hand stopped in the act of loosening his tie, and an eyebrow shot up.

She went on hurriedly, ''Everett's made arrangements for us to share breakfast, lunch, and dinners, and go to cocktail gatherings, openings, and parties. I tried to tell him that you don't go for that sort of thing, but he was—uh—fairly dogmatic about the whole thing. I hope you don't mind.''

His expression was enigmatic. He threw his tie on the back of the chair and unbuttoned the top three buttons of his light blue shirt.

''Will I have the pleasure of your company at all these functions?''

She was embarrassed. ''I'm afraid so.''

''Then I'm sure I'll find them delightful,'' he replied easily. ''What's on the agenda for tonight?''

''Just dinner. I persuaded him to forgo the private party at Studio 54 on the plea that you'd be suffering from jet lag. We can still go if you're dying to, though. Everett made me promise I'd let you know we were invited.''

''What's the party?'' Lawrence said, his expression inscrutable.

''It's for a designer—Solomon Arpeggio. He just made a mint on a new kind of suspender.'' Seeing his face, she broke into a laugh. "Forget it, believe me. It's not your kind of party."

He laughed too. "You're right. Dinner sounds fine, though. Will we have company?"

Nadine hesitated. "No," she said. "Just us. Everett—"

He interrupted impatiently. "Yes, I know. Everett ordered you, Everett made you promise, Everett thought, Everett said! I get the message. You don't want to have dinner with me, but he's forcing you to. What beats me is how he can force you, of all people, to do something you don't want to do."

She tried to make a joke out of his impatience and gave another laugh.

"Blackmail, of course." She dropped her eyes nervously. "We have reservations for seven-thirty. I'll come by here about seven. We're going to Tavern-on-the-Green. It'll be a nice walk through the park."

She wished he wouldn't eye her like that. Had Everett already informed him about the gallery opening he wanted them to attend at five o'clock, and was he waiting for her to mention it? She had planned on telling Everett in the morning that Lawrence didn't feel up to going to it. It was imperative that she see Jamie at least for a couple of hours this afternoon if she couldn't be with him all evening.

"Fine." His arms were folded, waiting for her to speak or leave or—something. She still hesitated, trying to decide whether or not she should mention the opening. "I assume you're longing to return to the gallery and be briefed by Everett on what you're supposed to say to me at dinner," he continued after a silence. "You are going back to the gallery, aren't you?"

Miserably, Nadine nodded. She hated lying.

He went to the bedroom door and opened it for her.

"I'll see you at seven," he said, smiling.

$$* \quad * \quad *$$

Nadine hesitated in front of the hotel, standing under the flapping awning, wondering what to do. She longed to see Jamie, but if Everett discovered that they had not gone to the gallery opening, and she had not returned to the office, would he carry out his threat and betray her secret to Lawrence? What would happen if Lawrence did find out about Jamie? At some moments she knew for a certainty that he would not do anything to separate her from him, but at other times her love for her son made her fearful. If Lawrence saw her dark, shabby apartment, the dingy block on which she lived, or if he learned about Jamie's unruliness in class and his increasingly difficult disposition, wouldn't he think it his duty to take Jamie away from New York? Not from her, exactly, but from the unhealthy atmosphere of the city.

She took a few paces toward the Mills Gallery, then hesitated again. If Everett told Lawrence about Jamie right away, he would lose his hold over her. It was unlikely that he would play his cards while she could still be useful to him. Besides, how would he know whether they had attended the gallery opening or not? She turned around abruptly and headed uptown toward her sister's.

Charlotte was furious at Everett's behavior, but her suggested solution to his blackmail was simple: tell Lawrence about Jamie so that Everett could no longer threaten her.

To Nadine's unhappy objection that she couldn't trust Lawrence not to take Jamie from her she uttered a scornful "Pshaw! A natural father would have no rights to the child over his mother!"

Nadine shook her head. "If the natural father happens to be extremely wealthy, famous, and determined, and the mother happens to be unwed, young, poor, and working outside the home, I can assure you the father has just as much chance of getting custody as the mother."

Steve, when he returned from work some time later, sided with Charlotte.

"You'll make yourself ill over the fear that he'll learn about Jamie some other way. And chances are he will, too. Tell him, Nadine. It'll make you feel a whole lot better."

But the most they could extract from her was a promise that she would consider it, and might tell him in a couple of days.

When Jamie heard that Mommy was going out for dinner without him, and that he would be spending the night at Auntie Charlotte's he had a fit of the sulks he had been displaying more and more frequently lately. He retreated to the guest bedroom, lying on the bed, drawing with colored crayons, and not looking up when Nadine came in to talk to him. She closed the door and sat on the edge of the bed.

"Jamie, darling," she began, fighting the crack in her voice at seeing his hurt obstinacy. "You know I have to work in order to make enough money for us to live. What I'm doing tonight is part of my work. You know I wouldn't leave you if I didn't have to. I'm going to miss you like crazy. You mustn't think it's because I want to go out that I'm leaving you."

"Where are you going?" he asked sullenly.

"Just to dinner. I won't be out late, and I'll come back here afterward and take you out for breakfast before school tomorrow." That meant two breakfasts, but there was no help for it. She was going to put on a lot of weight if Everett's scheme went through as he had planned. "We'll be just the two of us; we'll wake up bright and early, and then I'll walk you to school. How's that?"

"I don't want to stay here tonight. I want to go home."

Nadine stared at him helplessly, raging inwardly at Everett's callousness.

"Darling, I know you do. I do too. But sometimes in life you have to do things you don't want to do. We're in this together, Jamie, remember that. Look at it as though you're helping me with my job. And in less than a week this show

I'm doing will be over and we won't have to work so hard anymore. Okay?''

She saw that Jamie was fighting tears bravely, and took him in her arms, holding him tightly. He gulped back a sob.

"Okay, Mommy."

Charlotte loaned Nadine one of the evening dresses she had bought several years earlier when she had been slimmer.

"This one would look really nice," she suggested, taking out an emerald-green silk dress with a neckline that plunged to a V at the waist in front.

Nadine laughed. "This is a business dinner," she protested. "And my business is not getting Lawrence to bed. Let's see another one."

But Charlotte had a taste for sexy, flowing, designer dresses, and each one she brought out was more *risqué* than the last. With a reluctant sigh, Nadine slipped into the emerald silk and surveyed herself critically in the mirror.

"You look fabulous!" Charlotte exclaimed with delight. "It fits you perfectly! Oh, Nadine, why did I get fat?"

"You're not fat," Nadine protested, laughing. "You're cuddly, and you know Steve prefers you that way, so be grateful." She narrowed her eyes and spun gracefully around a few times. The soft material lifted gracefully around her knees and fell again in shimmering, lovely folds. Her bare throat was pale and swanlike when she lifted her chin, her shoulders continuing the graceful line. It was a lovely dress and Nadine was certain Steve had paid a fortune for it.

"I think I only wore it once," Charlotte said sadly. "What a waste!"

Nadine agreed, but said nothing. At least Lawrence would have no idea of her struggle with poverty when he saw her in this outfit. The thought of her meager wardrobe in the tiny closet at home made her want to giggle. That was something Lawrence would never see. Tonight she would be someone else—a mysterious and wealthy companion of the famous artist.

On her knees, Charlotte was scrounging around the closet floor for shoes.

"Your feet are bigger than mine," she gasped, finally finding what she was looking for. "But see if these will fit. You don't mind a blister or two for the sake of glamour, do you?"

Nadine slipped her feet into the high-heeled emerald pumps. They were simple, stylish, and a painful size too small. She winced.

"Never mind," Charlotte encouraged her. "You'll be sitting down eating most of the time, remember. No one will notice if you take them off. Here are a pair of nylons—they'll make them more comfortable. Now for a necklace." She left the room.

Nadine felt a sudden twinge of *déjà vu:* she and Charlotte could be teenagers again, setting off on a date. They used to exchange clothes and advise each other all the time, although as teenagers it had been Charlotte who had gotten most of the advice, for she went out most often. Nadine remained behind, chubby and affectionate, just as Charlotte was being tonight.

"Aha!" Charlotte reentered with a coral necklace in her hand. "Red and green! Perfect! How do you like it?"

Nadine shook her head, slipping her stockinged feet back into the pumps again, then hastily taking them off. "Very pretty, but I can't wear it. It's too like the one Lawrence gave me in Florence."

"Then pretend it's his. Look at that stunning color combination!"

"Nope. Sorry, Char. What else do you have?"

"Pearls?" she suggested doubtfully.

"Perfect. I'll look too sophisticated for him to speak to. Maybe I'll terrify him into silence."

The short string of glowing pearls hugged her throat, lying flat against her chest. The added height, the expensively simple silk dress, and the pearls combined to give her a not unwelcome sensation of luxury and sophistication.

"Want to use my makeup? I'm going to check up on our dinner. It won't be as good as yours, but I have to keep doing my best."

"Atta girl, Char," Nadine replied absently, heading for the makeup box on top of the bureau. She rarely wore makeup, but tonight she was more daring than usual. Mascara darkened her thick eyelashes, and faint green eyeshadow echoed the green of her dress. She tinted her pale cheeks with blush. Then she brushed her hair but restrained an impulse to put it up. It would never stay in any other way but with the side parting, a thick wave falling across one eye to her shoulders. She dabbed some Joy perfume behind her ears and stood up, trying to imagine Lawrence's reaction. For a moment she wondered why she was dressing up with such care for him. She frowned. It was fun, that was all. She hadn't been out on a date for years; she hadn't dressed up, hadn't had the opportunity to giggle with her sister and share her clothes. She was enjoying it.

A faint smile on her lips, she entered the living room. Steve gave a long whistle.

"I don't know what you're setting out to do," he told her, "but whatever it is, you'll do it. You look terrific!"

She smiled dazzlingly.

"Thanks."

"Drink before you go?"

"It's quarter to seven. I'd better be going, I think. I said I'd pick up Lawrence at seven."

Charlotte, on hearing Steve's exclamation, came into the room, an apron tied around her waist. She gazed approvingly at her sister.

"You look terrific, sis. If you start feeling depressed, just look in the mirror. Are you coming back here tonight?"

Nadine nodded. "I'll sleep on the couch, if that's all right. I promised Jamie I'd take him out for an early breakfast so we could have some time together alone. We'll probably be gone before you wake up." She picked up her gray cardigan. Steve had already phoned for a cab.

Luxuriating in the feel of silk against her body and the warm September breeze against her face, Nadine leaned back against the soft backseat of the taxi as it sped down Fifth Avenue to the Pierre. It had been a long time since she had had the luxury of even a taxi. Everett would receive every single bill she footed entertaining Lawrence, including all taxis. She remembered to ask for a receipt before alighting at the hotel.

"Please tell Mr. Lawrence Stebbing that Nadine Barnet is here," she asked the receptionist, ignoring his admiring look. She turned her back to the desk as he called Lawrence's room, and gazed around at the elegant lobby, feeling a secret excitement beneath her dignified facade. Lawrence, Lawrence! she sang in her breast. I'm going out with Lawrence!

"He would like you to come upstairs to his room," the receptionist interrupted her thoughts. "It's number 1206."

She had been expecting that he would come downstairs and they would set off immediately, but she did not want to argue with the receptionist. No doubt Lawrence had fallen asleep and had only just woken up. Now she would have to wait for him to get ready. The thought that he hadn't been impatiently waiting for her arrival irked her.

He opened the door the moment she knocked, very much as though he had been impatiently waiting for her. He eyed her appraisingly, his mouth firmly closed, and stepped aside to let her in. Casually she dropped her purse and cardigan on the nearest chair and walked gracefully toward the desk by the open window. She took in nothing for a few seconds while she tried to calm her thumping heart. Then she turned around.

He stood in the middle of the room, hands in his pants pockets, regarding her quizzically. His black suit jacket was cut to perfection on his shoulders, and the black pants accentu-

ated his long legs. His shirt dazzled her with its whiteness; a
burgundy silk tie completed the distinguished-looking attire.

"Hi," he said.

She offered him a smile. Why had she expected him to be
unshaven, half dressed, and hung over?

"You look terrific. Have a seat?"

Reluctantly Nadine dragged her eyes away from his intent
ones and sat in the red velvet armchair. Only then did she
notice the bottle of champagne and two champagne glasses on
the coffee table. She lifted her eyes back to Lawrence.

"Celebrating your return?"

He looked surprised. "I thought you were responsible.
This arrived about ten minutes ago. Welcoming my return, if
you like. You mean you didn't have it sent up?"

She shook her head. "It must be courtesy of the hotel."

"I don't think so." He picked up a large card from the
desk and handed it to her. "Whose writing is that?"

It was the typical Mills Gallery promotional piece that
Donna kept on her receptionist's desk to hand out or send to
whoever might be interested in a particular show. Nadine did
not look at the front, but read the back announcement of
Lawrence's upcoming exhibition and the scrawled message
written across it: "Welcome back to New York." Everett, of
course.

"Everett." She spoke the name out loud.

"You've seen the card before?" Why was his voice so
peculiar? She glanced up.

"He makes these up for specific shows and sends them
around to anyone who might help in making them a success."
Carelessly she turned the card over to see which of Lawrence's
paintings he'd chosen to advertise the exhibition. He had
allowed her no say in the matter, and she had not pressed for
it. Now she saw why.

She relived again the sweeping nostalgia when she had
seen this same painting in Lawrence's studio a month earlier.
Again she was staring at herself; younger, vulnerable, filled

with love and satiated desire. A deep crimson spread over her face this time, however, not the aching pallor that had overtaken her last time.

She was surprised at the steadiness of her voice. "I didn't know he was going to use that picture for promotional purposes. I didn't think—"

But why shouldn't he use it? she asked herself tiredly. They had all agreed it was Lawrence's best painting. A man like Everett would not allow her feelings to interfere with the success of the show, as he himself had made clear.

"I assumed you'd be in charge of this sort of thing." Lawrence was nonplussed by her reaction. That she had not seen the card before was evident.

"Usually I am." Nadine dropped the card on the table and met his eyes again, trying to put the painting out of her mind. How could a mere reproduction of a canvas reduce her to quivering jelly? How could she remember so vividly her feelings when the painting had been created? "This time Everett insisted that he handle the publicity. He thought it was too important to allow me the chance to screw it up. Now I see why. I'd never have chosen this painting."

Lawrence took the chilled bottle from the silver ice bucket and started easing off the cork.

"Why not?" he grunted. "It's one of my better efforts."

She did not reply directly. "Yes, it is, isn't it?"

The cork flew off with a bang, and champagne frothed onto the carpet. Deftly, Lawrence filled the glasses.

"To Everett Mills," he suggested, handing her a glass.

She assented in silence, and took a demure sip. Unfortunately she swallowed the wrong way and began to choke. Hastily she set down the glass and gasped for air. A hard slap on her back made her laugh.

"Thanks," she said when she could breathe. "It went down the wrong way. Let's make another toast. Maybe it'll work better. To a successful show. Let's see if I choke on that one." She sipped it gingerly and Lawrence returned her smile, drinking with her.

Because it was almost eight when they had finished the champagne and were ready to leave, they decided to get a cab instead of walking to the restaurant. Nadine gave a silent sigh of relief, knowing that her poor feet would be devastated by the short walk through the park in her sister's shoes. While they stood waiting for the doorman to whistle down a cab, not touching, she replied to Lawrence's questions with only one ear. The other ear was reveling in the music of the traffic and lively conversations of the people milling in front of the hotel. This was a side of New York she had glimpsed but never thought to be a part of, or even wanted to. It was just for one night, or a few days possibly, then she would return to her everyday life. But while she had the opportunity she would enjoy this to its fullest. They settled in the back seat of the taxi, not too close to each other, talking amicably.

It was wonderful to be with him again. Aside from the fact that he evinced no romantic interest in her, he was the Lawrence she remembered from four years ago: interested, alert, humorous, sympathetic. She was reminded of the occasions when they'd gone to the opera in Florence, or to a concert. But then there had been a warm glow in his eyes, and his hand rarely left hers. That was the only difference, she told herself firmly, a minor one.

They were shown with deference to their table outside in the garden lit by lanterns strung from the trees. Nadine was enchanted.

"Do you come here often?" Lawrence asked when they had ordered.

"No." Her sophisticated cloak fell slightly. "First time, as a matter of fact."

He lifted his brows. "Everyone seems to know who you are, though. How could that be?"

She had not noticed anything out of the ordinary other than the extreme courtesy they had been shown.

"I don't know," she responded, wondering why Lawrence was frowning. The brief illumination from a camera flash lit their table, and she followed Lawrence's eyes to the back of the restaurant. Two photographers and a reporter headed toward them. She looked back at Lawrence in alarm.

"What have you—" he began threateningly.

Surely he did not think that she had set up a press conference at his first dinner! How could he imagine her so thoughtless, so rude!

"Good evening." The man with the notebook had actually dared to approach them. "I hope you don't mind my interrupting. I'm Les Stein from the *Herald Times*. Welcome back to New York, Mr. Stebbing. Are you planning on staying here for a while?"

Nadine intervened before Lawrence could reply. She had issued an invitation, albeit on Everett's orders, and Lawrence's privacy and comfort were her responsibility. She spoke curtly. "Mr. Stebbing will be holding a scheduled press conference while he is in New York, and you can ask him what you like at that time. He isn't answering any questions tonight."

Instead of being rebuffed, the man shifted his attention to Nadine. Aware of the clicking cameras around her, she made an effort not to glower. A quick glance at Lawrence gave her no satisfaction: his expression was enigmatic.

"Yes, Miss Barnet. It's very nice to meet you too. Is it true that you acted as a live-in muse for Mr. Stebbing several years ago, and that's when he painted some of his finest work? Why did you walk out on him? May I take it from this intimate dinner party that your relationship is back on the footing it was when Mr. Stebbing painted *Tuscan Dawn*?"

Just as Nadine was about to lose her temper, Lawrence intervened.

"Ms. Barnet will be at the press conference with me. Any questions can be addressed to her then. Now if you'll excuse us, we'd like to be left alone for our dinner."

Aware that everyone in the restaurant garden was looking

at them, Nadine writhed in anger. To her relief she saw the maître d' make his way over to their table in answer to the curt gesture Lawrence made.

"We wish to have privacy," he informed him. "Please escort these gentlemen out of the restaurant."

The authoritative voice had dealt with annoyingly persistent journalists before now, and the maître d' sensed that if the journalists weren't made to leave, Mr. Stebbing himself would. Hastily he ushered the clicking cameramen out the door. Lawrence regarded Nadine's flushed face sympathetically.

"You don't have to tell me," he said. "Everett—"

She nodded, not speaking.

"I'm looking forward very much to meeting this man," he remarked dryly, making an effort to resume the close companionship of a few moments earlier. "I don't remember him as being so tyrannical and publicity-hungry."

"Well, he is." She was ashamed and embarrassed for Lawrence. It was awful that he should be submitted to an ordeal like this on his first day back in the United States. How could Everett be so thoughtless? But why did she think he would be less thoughtless to Lawrence then he was to her?

"Hey." She glanced up and met his eyes. "You're not upset, are you?"

"Of course I'm upset," she retorted indignantly. "He had no right to do that! I know you've always hated scenes like that, and I told him so. I should have known it would make no difference."

"It makes no difference to me," he assured her quietly. "Let's forget about it, okay? I've had to handle worse questions than those before now. Besides, I've matured." He gave her a wink. "I don't lose my temper as easily as I used to."

The food arrived, and they turned their attention to the meal. Delicate stars overhead cloaked their intimacy in velvet-dark enchantment, and Nadine again was lost in the strange, secret sweetness of being with Lawrence again.

"Tell me about Everett," Lawrence asked at last.

They had covered a wide variety of topics: books they'd recently read, movies they'd seen, politics; all abstract, impersonal subjects—as they ate their way through scallops and crab and salad.

Before Nadine replied to his question the maître d' came to their table with two glasses of brandy.

"On the house," he informed them. "With apologies for the earlier intrusion."

Thanking him, Lawrence sniffed the brandy appreciatively.

"Won't do any more damage than has already been done," he said and grinned at her. Although a little light-headed, Nadine did not feel drunk. She smiled back and breathed the aromatic liquor.

"Everett," she said slowly. "I don't think I can say anything about him. It wouldn't be fair."

An eyebrow rose. "What do you mean?"

She grinned. "It would be unprofessional of me to slander my employer to the artist whose work we're going to exhibit. I'd better not say anything at all."

"Ah." He took another sip. "That was all I really wanted to know. Now answer me another question. Why do you work at his gallery if you don't care for him?"

"I need the job."

"May I ask how much you make?"

She shook her head, smiling. "Sorry, no. I don't want you to break your heart over my rotten salary." She added gloomily, "It'll probably come out in the gossip columns that'll carry our story these next few days, so don't be upset." She paused. "Lawrence, you look exhausted. It must be almost morning for you on your schedule. Let me take you back to your hotel. Remember we're having breakfast tomorrow."

"Spare me." He grinned.

"I wish I could spare myself too, but at least that means we won't have to be at Everett's office till eleven."

"What time did Everett"—he emphasized the name distastefully—"make our reservation for?"

"Nine o'clock, at your hotel. We can walk to the gallery from there." As long as she was wearing her other shoes, she thought ruefully, feeling her toes crying in vexation under the table.

Lawrence did not answer at once, and the waiter brought them the exorbitant check. He reached for it, but her small hand stayed his.

"Everett will pay for this," she informed him.

"In more ways than one, I imagine from your tone," he replied dryly, allowing her to take the check from him.

It was only once they were in a taxi again and heading to his hotel that Lawrence told her:

"I don't know what game Everett is up to, and I'm not sure that you do, but I'm willing to go along with him until I find out. So nine o'clock it is, in my hotel. Meet in the lobby?"

"Okay." Gratefully she slipped out of the too-tight shoes and leaned her head back. The cab bounced over a pothole, and her head was knocked against the seat.

"Ouch," she exclaimed.

He moved nearer to her. The gauntness of his face was marked in the passing streetlights, and the sockets of his eyes remained in deep shadow so she could not tell their expression. But he slipped his arm around her. "Put your head here on my shoulder. Is that more comfortable?"

It was, in a way, but the strong, comforting circle of his arm around her and the scent of after-shave that he used affected her peculiarly in another way. Her cheek rested on the smooth material of the jacket and she closed her eyes. If only . . .

The ride to his hotel was too short. She hated being parted from him, and reluctantly lifted her head from his shoulder.

"Everett's going to pay." She restrained him again from taking out his wallet. "Besides, I'm taking the cab uptown."

His eyes were still black sockets: she could not tell if he was disappointed or relieved or indifferent. But he put a hand to her chin and lifted her mouth to his for one brief, exquisite moment. His lips were soft, the kiss a promise, not a demand. He released her almost immediately and got out.

"Nine o'clock," he reminded her, leaning in the half-open window. "Good night."

"Good night."

The dazzling light from the hotel lobby caught his eyes as he swung around and went up the shallow stairs to the entrance. Her heart thudded as the taxi sped off again. The glimpse she'd had of those narrow, deep-set eyes revealed to her that Lawrence was neither disappointed nor relieved nor indifferent. His expression had been one of unmistakable desire.

Chapter Seven

The next morning Nadine stormed into Everett's office, threw her purse on the chair by his desk, and stood in front of him, her hands on her hips, her eyes flashing.

"What in hell's name to you mean by setting a pack of gossip columnists on our tail, hounding Lawrence out of his mind, and humiliating me even more? Where'd they get the story of our affair? From you! How'd they know what time his plane was arriving, where we were eating last night and this morning? You! Why'd they assume we'd slept together last night? Because you arranged for us to have breakfast in Lawrence's hotel so that it would look as though we had resumed our affair! Good God, Everett, don't you have any sense of decency?"

"Take it easy," he drawled, failing to hide his delight in the success of his plan. "Where is Lawrence Stebbing now?"

"He stopped downstairs to pick up a paper. I said I wanted a word with you first. Everett, Lawrence doesn't want this kind of trashy publicity, get it? He doesn't want to be annoyed by offensive questions, get it? He doesn't want to be seen with me in order to get a higher price for his wretched paintings, get it? You're going about this entirely the wrong way. If I were Lawrence I'd withdraw from the show immediately! And I'm certainly going to withdraw from these disgusting duties you forced on me. If I'd known why you asked me to hang around with Lawrence I would have refused when you first asked me.''

"We both know why you wouldn't have refused me anything,'' Everett replied, his eyes glittering. "Don't start acting indignant at this late date, sweetie. Instead you'd better give me a damned good reason why you didn't show up at the gallery opening yesterday afternoon. The press weren't pleased about being sent there on a wild-goose chase.''

"I'm glad!'' In the height of her temper, Nadine didn't care what she said. "You have no right to do this!''

Everett leaned forward and spat out the words viciously:

"Now you get this, Nadine Barnet: You work for me, and you are not in a position to tell me how to run my business. Get that? I won't tolerate rudeness, bad manners, or a shirking of your responsibilities. Get that? I want to hear your reason for not showing up at the opening.''

"Lawrence didn't want to go.'' Nadine struggled with her temper. How she hated this smug, offensive man!

"Next time you'll make him go, Nadine. I won't betray your secret this time, but don't count on my generosity if you fail me again. I mean it. I'll use whatever means I have to make this show a success. You happen to be that means.''

"He'll pull out,'' Nadine retorted confidently. "You'll see. Maybe I can be blackmailed, but he can't. He won't stand for this sort of treatment.''

Everett shrugged indifferently. "If he pulls out, you lose your job, your sole means of support, Nadine. I'm counting on you to persuade him not to be rash. Furthermore, if he pulls out you can be sure both he and the press will learn about your—''

He had been going to say "child,'' but Nadine's cry interrupted him before he had uttered the word. She had turned away from the desk, frustrated and furious, and seen that Lawrence, unseen by them both, had been standing in the doorway listening. How much he had heard of their conversation she could not tell from his expression.

"Everett," she said, forcing herself to calm down. "Here's Lawrence."

A smile oiled Everett's face, and he stood up and held out his hand.

"Lawrence Stebbing. Such a pleasure to see you at last. Nadine has been telling me about some trouble you encountered over breakfast? I hope you weren't too put out by it. Reporters, you know. They simply won't leave one alone!" He clucked his tongue sympathetically.

Nadine glowered.

"I understand." Lawrence responded to Everett's proffered hand with his own.

"I'm sorry you didn't feel up to attending Uptho's opening yesterday evening. It was quite an event." Everett motioned him into a chair.

"Uptho?" Lawrence inquired politely, sitting down and glancing at Nadine.

She explained hastily, mute appeal in her gray eyes: "The opening you didn't feel like going to before dinner." How would she explain this to him later?

He came to her rescue, seemingly unperturbed.

"Oh, right. I really was much too exhausted to face Uptho right after getting off the plane."

The matters they touched on after that related purely to business, which Everett handled with a swift, smooth expertise. No matter how much she disliked him, his business sense never failed to impress Nadine. Lawrence reclined in the chair he was given, hands in his gray pants pockets, his jacket on. He had not worn a tie, and his white shirt was unbuttoned at the throat, exposing the top few hairs on his chest. They gave Nadine an odd feeling of intimacy, regarding them secretly, as though Lawrence were on her side, and would back her to the hilt no matter what. Lawrence did not seem overly enthusiastic about any of Everett's ideas, however, and coolly informed him of several changes he wished to see made. Gratified, Nadine saw that none her own arrangements were affected.

Why didn't she trust him to leave her and Jamie alone if she told him about his son? she wondered, as the men argued about the price for one of Lawrence's more recent water colors. That he had let her down once was not a good enough reason. She decided she would find out his true feelings about being a father before she told him of her son's existence. Somehow she had to get out of Everett's clutches and spend more time with Jamie.

But as soon as they had exited from the gallery and set off toward Mercurio's for lunch, Lawrence spoke bitingly to Nadine:

"So that's your smitten Everett Mills. You two seem to have an extraordinary relationship."

"What do you mean?" His cutting voice had banished the camaraderie and intimacy she had felt in the office.

His jaw was set. "What did he mean when he said you wouldn't refuse him anything?"

So he *had* overheard! Nadine's heart sank, and she had to skip to match his long strides. She glanced at his drawn brows and tensed, grim mouth, feeling farther from him than ever. Unable to lie, she did not reply.

They entered the elegant Italian restaurant and were seated at a table near the window. The waiter took their order and left them. Lawrence settled back in his chair and sipped a gin and tonic.

"Last night you didn't want to talk about your boss because you didn't want to slander him to me. Now that I've met him, would you mind answering some questions about him?"

"It depends on the questions." She gave him a half-smile that did not reach her eyes.

"He seems very anxious to keep you on staff," he said sarcastically. "Is he usually so concerned about your welfare?"

Of course he had overheard Everett threatening to fire her

if Lawrence pulled out of the show, she realized. She spoke slowly: "He is concerned about me, in a way, and he's a good businessman, obviously, or Mills Gallery wouldn't be the success it is. I just don't always agree with his methods of handling the business—for instance submitting you to gossip columnists and cameras wherever we go. He didn't take kindly to my criticism and lost his temper." She gazed back at him levelly.

He was in no hurry to remove his eyes from hers.

"I see. He lost his temper when you told him you refused to go along with his plan of having us seen in public together all the time, is that it?"

"That's it."

"Then he said that you both knew why you wouldn't refuse him anything. Will you let me in on the reason?"

She ran a tongue over her dry lips. "I need the job," she replied.

"Of course you do." His voice was cool as the blade of a knife. "Now, let's see. Yesterday when I asked you why Everett could force you to take on responsibilities that you disliked you mentioned blackmail. Funny that that word's been mentioned twice in two days, isn't it?"

She took a sip of dry white wine to soothe her dry throat. "Well, it's true." She tried to sound relaxed. "I just told you: I need this job. Do you know what the cost of living is in New York now?"

"I don't think it's a particularly relevant point just now," he replied smoothly. "A woman of your intelligence and experience could surely find another place to work."

She raised her eyebrows and tried to look patronizing.

"Don't tell me you haven't been reading the papers since you left the United States! Haven't you heard that our unemployment rate is the highest it's been since the Depression? I've been looking for another position for almost a year, I assure you."

He was unimpressed by the eyebrows. "I'm glad to hear

that. But you still haven't answered my question. What on earth can your boss use to blackmail you with?''

"I told you: threatening to fire me.''

"Is that the 'secret' he promised not to betray? How disappointing. I thought maybe you'd murdered someone or robbed a bank.''

"That's the secret,'' she replied firmly. Her hand shook when she picked up the wineglass again.

"You're a lousy liar.'' He sounded disgusted.

Nadine concentrated her eyes on the patch of curly black hair above the line of his shirt, trying with no success to regain that comforting sense of intimacy that she had felt sitting in Everett's office. How could she have imagined that she might be able to confide her fears and insecurities to this man? Much less tell him about Jamie! There was no way of reaching him when he looked like this. A liar! He had called her a liar!

"Don't start acting indignant with me, either,'' Lawrence recalled Everett's words again. "You're only getting yourself in deeper water. Now, look at this from my viewpoint. I'm overwhelmed with curiosity about this little 'secret' you're sharing with your boss. He did say if I pulled out of the show I'd learn about it, didn't he? And the press too. You interrupted him before he got a chance to reveal exactly what it was that I'd learn, unfortunately. But he did give me a way of finding out.''

The blood drained from her face. He would pull out of the show; Everett would fire her; Lawrence would learn about Jamie; she would have no means to fight him for custody; and she would lose them both—Jamie and Lawrence. As the thoughts flashed through her mind, an unwelcome diversion was occuring in the front of the restaurant, and to her dismay, Nadine saw more reporters heading toward them. She stood up abruptly, unable to face any more damning questions.

"Nadine, wait.'' Lawrence's voice changed. The exit was blocked by the journalists, and Nadine suddenly didn't have

the strength to push through them. She slipped into the ladies'
room and leaned against the sink, grateful to find herself
alone. The room was mercifully silent and cool. She wondered how Lawrence was handling himself with the reporters
and smiled wryly. It served him right to have to face them by
himself, after threatening to pull out of the show and thus
cause her to lose her job. The fact that Lawrence seemed to
have sided with Everett in this affair, against her, filled her
with deep disappointment. He could have been her ally; and
if he had inspired her with trust, he could have been told
about Jamie and this entire charade could be dropped. A
woman entered and Nadine went through the motions of
fixing her hair. It was time to go out and face the music, she
decided at last. She'd been in there too long already.

Lawrence was sitting by himself at the table, sipping a
fresh cocktail. There was no sign of the newspaperman's cameras
and notebooks. He stared at the glass in his hands, swirling the
ice, lost in thought. Nadine approached the table slowly. He
glanced up.

"Hi. You missed an entertaining little skirmish." When
she said nothing, he asked, "What's on the agenda for this
afternoon?"

"You're free to do whatever you'd like," she replied
coldly, hating the veil of frost that had settled between them
but powerless to lift it.

"Are we having dinner again tonight?"

"Unfortunately, yes. After cocktails with Everett in the
Rainbow Room."

Lawrence made a face so ridiculous that Nadine had to
struggle to hide her laughter. When they had left the restaurant he walked her back to the gallery, proposing to do some
gallery-hopping around SoHo on his own during the afternoon.
Outside her building he pulled her to the side of the white
stone wall and rested his hands on her shoulders in a way she
remembered well. He looked down at her.

"I don't know what you and Everett are up to," Lawrence

said carefully. "Your schemes and your secrets are beyond my comprehension, and I can see I'm not going to get anything out of either of you in the way of explanations. But I'm not going to pull out of the show to get them. I don't want to be responsible for losing you your job. I'll find out, but I'll find out my way. I'll find out what hold Everett has over you, why you work for him in the first place, and why you follow orders that disgust you. I'll find out why you didn't mention the art opening I was supposed to go to yesterday and why you lied to Everett about my being too exhausted to attend." When she did not enlighten him he continued, "But there's more to it than that. I want to find out where you live, and see your apartment." Here Nadine blanched visibly. "And I want to meet your parents and your sister. I want to find out what's been going on with you these past four years. Do you understand? So I'll go along with the charade, assuming that by doing so I'm protecting your job, but in return I want answers. All the answers—eventually." He leaned down further and brushed his lips to hers. Nadine experienced a slight shock when their lips met, then her eyes closed and she yielded herself to the firm, assertive mouth.

"It's strange," he muttered at last, his mouth half an inch from hers, "your kisses are the least secret thing about you. I wonder what I could learn from kissing you instead of talking to you." He held her chin between thumb and forefinger, making it impossible to look away. "What time should I meet you at the Rainbow Room?"

"Six-thirty," she replied, a little breathlessly.

He released her, and she turned abruptly away and headed for the elevator at the far end of the lobby, but not before she heard another familiar click of a camera.

During the next few days Nadine swung alternately between periods of dizzying rapture and pressing anxiety. The regular appearance of reporters and photographers grew exhausting, but Everett refused to give in to her plea for privacy. Weekly gossip magazines managed to get hold of photographs of her and Lawrence in a variety of intimate settings. The daily papers carried an almost constant report of their activities, and Nadine had been approached by several women's magazines for an interview to discuss the truth behind the romantic tale.

"Four years was a long time to be separated from the man she loves, but Nadine Barnet did not give up hope. She arranged for the famous Lawrence Stebbing to hold an exhibition at the gallery where she works. The flames of their passion have rekindled from when these two lovers lived together in Florence, four years ago. Since arriving in New York, our distinguished artist is seldom seen apart from the gallery worker, proving that Barnet's perseverance in regaining the man she loves has been successful. We know one of the paintings to be shown at the exhibition is a testament to their torrid romance."

Nadine cringed when she read this paragraph in one of the gossip columns she thumbed through and hoped Lawrence wouldn't come across it. When Charlotte handed her the latest issue of a paper with the photograph of her kissing Lawrence outside the gallery, she blushed. Charlotte looked inquisitive.

"It doesn't look as though you hate him as much as you say you do," she pointed out. "What is going on between you two? I've read so much garbage lately that I can't sift out facts from fiction."

But Nadine could not be prevailed upon to elaborate on the newspaper reports. She told her sister only that Everett insisted she continue chaperoning Lawrence around New York, but they had not gotten emotionally involved again.

Disbelieving, Charlotte glanced again at the photograph.

"Are you going to tell him about Jamie?"

"Jamie!" she exclaimed. "Are you kidding? Those blasted reporters would surround him when he came out of school, when he left in the morning . . . he'd never get a moment's peace, Char! I'm just grateful and amazed they haven't found out about him already.''

"I'm not suggesting you tell the reporters about him.'' Charlotte was unimpressed by Nadine's vehemence. "Just his father. It's his right to know.''

Nadine gave a harsh laugh. "You think if the three of us were seen walking around New York together those reporters wouldn't jump on us like a pack of wolves? I won't submit Jamie to that—I find it hard enough myself.''

"Oh, Nadine,'' Charlotte responded sympathetically. "You are having a hard time of it, aren't you? But as soon as the opening is over you'll have more freedom, less pressure. Maybe you can tell him then.''

To this she made no reply. Everett had informed her earlier that day that he was tempted to ''accidentally'' reveal the fact that Lawrence had a son in order to ensure the show's success. She had fought hard with him, resorting to lies and threats in order to persuade him to remain silent on that score as he initially promised he would. She told him that she and Lawrence were deeply involved again, and she was only waiting until after the show's opening to tell him about Jamie. If Everett subjected Lawrence's son to the press Lawrence would be furious, she assured him. He would pull out of the show without a second thought. Everett pursed his lips and agreed to keep the secret awhile longer.

The night before the opening, Nadine was unusually thoughtful. She and Lawrence had taken a cab to Little Italy and were strolling around the narrow, gaily lit streets after dinner with quiet enjoyment. Lawrence tried again to learn more about her private life. She gave him monosyllabic responses, and when he asked again why she couldn't invite him to her apartment she withdrew still further, remembering Jamie's little room and the drab block on which she lived. Why did she never talk about her parents anymore? he persisted as they turned on Mulberry Street and walked past a shadowy children's playground. Again she replied shortly that she and her parents had had a fight and she never saw them.

She allowed him to take her hand after dinner that night, however, and as they walked up through SoHo her silence was more thoughtful than aloof. There was a faint crisp chill in the air, heralding the arrival of cold, wintry winds. He felt her shiver.

"I hate winter," she said suddenly.

Impulsively he put his arm around her shoulders, warming her. She stiffened, but the feel of his arm was too comforting and generous to repulse, and several paces later she slipped her own arm around his waist.

When they reached Washington Square they were tired enough to hail a cab. They settled in the back, Nadine leaning her head against Lawrence's shoulder, his arm still wrapped around her. Outside his hotel he asked:

"Want to come upstairs?"

The temptation was almost more than she could bear. His warmth, and his kindness made her long for him with a desire she dared not show. She shook her head. Jamie: she had to return to him. Besides, she told herself, she no longer wanted to have an affair with a man—any man. It hurt too much when it was over.

"See you tomorrow, then."

She smiled at him. "It'll be a huge success. Good night."

Chapter Eight

Cameras flashed, limousines pulled up on the wide street outside, pedestrians gathered around trying to learn what the occasion was, and the hum of conversation rose and fell like an orchestra readying itself for a concert. The men were in black tie, the women wore cocktail dresses, and everyone getting out of a limousine was approached by reporters and flashing cameras. If Everett had wanted sensational press coverage he was getting it now, Nadine thought to herself.

Safe inside the gallery, Nadine greeted arrivals with her lovely smile and kept her eyes on the refreshment table of champagne and cucumber sandwiches, making sure that everything was replenished promptly. She held a glass of champagne in one hand, sipped it occasionally, and exchanged pleasantries with those people she knew and greeted others she didn't know but who were curious about her much-publicized romance with the famous artist.

Tonight she was wearing white—a chiffon gown of Charlotte's, held by two thin straps over bare shoulders, and fully exposing her beautifully sculpted back. Charlotte had bought her thin silver stockings to wear with the white high heels, as a gift for the opening celebration. They felt luxuriously exotic on her slim legs, and more than once Nadine glanced at them with satisfaction.

The painting creating the most stir was *Tuscan Dawn*,

naturally. A crowd was constantly around it, and several offers had been made for it, all of which were turned down firmly. Lawrence had given instructions: The painting was not for sale, at any price.

Nadine was at Lawrence's side a good part of the evening, introducing him to potential buyers and several art critics, and sharing his private jokes.

"Mrs. Addamson, let me introduce you to Lawrence Stebbing. Lawrence, Mrs. Addamson has a private collection of considerable renown. She's very impressed with your work and wants some advice on which would be, in your opinion, a worthy purchase for her."

With an answering twinkle in his eye, Lawrence slipped the elderly woman's thin arm through his and offered to give her a personal inspection of his work. Nadine felt a surge of affection for this famous, brilliant artist whom everyone wished to know. Excitement and happiness made her suddenly breathless. She had forgotten she could feel this joy that used to well up in her unexpectedly when she was a girl. Her eyes followed his dark suit, the dragon-red tie, the crisp white shirt. His broad shoulders made Mrs. Addamson's elfin figure seem all the more reedlike. She was called away from his retreating figure by Everett.

"We've done it. A roaring success. I congratulate you."

"Thanks. You too." In a moment like this she felt generous even to the man who had treated her so shamefully. Everything was blissful. Her heart bounded against her breast, as though her physical body was too small to contain such a wealth of happiness. Tomorrow she would be plain old Nadine again; tonight, she was a celebrity. She was fully aware of the discreet glances, and covert murmurs and the stories that were being passed around about her. But tonight she did not mind the whispers or curious looks; she enjoyed them.

She saw Lawrence edging his way toward her again, and her heart leaped in anticipation. What was she doing? she thought wildly for a moment. Was she losing control of the tight reins she had kept on her feelings? No, she ordered herself firmly: It's just tonight that I'm feeling like this. I've been swept away by the excitement. Tomorrow everything will be normal again.

His smile touched her. "I'm glad I found you again. You're my haven from all these strangers." She remembered how much he disliked crowds and smiled back sympathetically.

"You're doing terrifically. No one can understand why you've had a reputation for being an ogre about exhibiting your work."

"Tell them it's because you weren't around to take care of the exhibitions.. You've done a great job." His eyes were warm. "And you're beautiful tonight, Nadine. Something's happened to make you look radiant."

She blushed. "It's all these people talking about me and looking at me while they pretend not to," she said lightly. "I must say I'm enjoying it in a funny sort of way."

"You thought your sister might be able to come," he said.

"Yes." Nadine had been glad of Charlotte's arrival, but she hadn't seen her since she disappeared into the room with the controversial painting, and she was apprehensive about her reaction to it.

"I'd like to meet her."

She could not refuse him anything that night, Nadine realized. His words touched her heart with wings, his touch on her elbow tugged at her excited pulse. How incredibly lucky she was to have known this man's love, she thought. She flashed him her disarming smile and led him into the large main room.

If she was worried about Charlotte's reception of Lawrence, her fears were set aside as soon as her eyes lighted on her sister. Charlotte hurried toward them, any hostility she harbored against Lawrence banished for that evening. She smiled warmly at him and held out her hand.

"I was just going to ask Nadine to introduce us," she told him, to Nadine's surprise.

"Charlotte, Lawrence. Lawrence, Charlotte," Nadine put in dutifully, amazed by Charlotte's flirtatious manner with the man she had professed to hate for her sister's sake. Charlotte teased him about a couple of his paintings, flattered him without fawning, and remarked on Nadine's reserve in talking about his work. At this Nadine frowned slightly. Charlotte changed the subject hastily.

"Steven, that's my husband, wasn't able to come tonight because he had to baby-sit our children. But I would like you two to meet." Again Nadine frowned and looked around the room, reluctant to hear Charlotte talking to Lawrence. What was she trying to do?

"Excuse me," she murmured and glided toward the refreshment table. There really wasn't anything for her to do: Champagne flowed like water; an exquisite variety of sandwiches lined the silver platters; there were no dirty glasses on the white tablecloth. She stared at the table, thinking. She had asked Lawrence several days ago when he was planning on returning to Florence, and he had hedged his answer. "When I discover your and Everett's secret," he'd replied with a determined gleam in his eyes. She had laughed, wondering if she would tell him.

"I finally understand how you could have lost your heart to that man," Charlotte said, coming up behind her and selecting a full glass of champagne. She gave an exaggerated sigh. "If only I weren't married! I knew I should have held off."

Nadine had to laugh at Charlotte's comical expression.

"I'm forgiven my sins?" She laughed shyly. "Think Mom'd understand if she met him?"

"Oh, Nadine." Charlotte squeezed her hand sympathetically. "She'd have to."

Nadine shrugged. Why were they talking about her mother on a night like this? "What'd you two talk about?"

"This and that. He really admires you. I'm beginning to have my doubts about whether your leaving him was really he best solution to your problems. I wonder if you're as much or more to blame for the separation as he was.''

She shrugged again. "Not more, anyway.''

"I've asked him for dinner tomorrow night," Charlotte went on. "I'd like him to meet Steve, and I know this will be my only chance to get to know the man who stole my sister's heart. He was delighted by the invitation; don't think I was too forward." Her eyes were mirthful when they encountered Nadine's horrified ones.

"But Charlotte, what about Jamie?" Her voice was low, urgent.

Finishing her champagne with a gulp, Charlotte reassured her, "He'll be in bed way before Lawrence arrives, and you know he usually sleeps like a top. There's no reason for Lawrence to find out about him. Although," she added speculatively, "you ought to tell him."

"I bet this is a plot you've hatched with Steve," Nadine replied. "Lawrence is probably in it too. I can't trust anyone!"

"You can't?" Lawrence came up behind her. "That's too bad."

Nadine veiled the apprehension in her eyes.

"Charlotte tells me she's asked you for dinner."

"If you'd only introduced me to her when I first arrived in New York I would have made sure the invitation was issued a while ago. I'm heartily sick of restaurants, despite the pleasure of your company at them." His relaxed voice covered up the tense moment.

"I have to leave." Charlotte smiled brightly at Lawrence. She held out her hand. "See you tomorrow."

"I'm looking forward to it," he replied courteously. "Goodnight, Charlotte. It's been a pleasure meeting you."

Charlotte kissed her sister and departed. Left alone with Lawrence, Nadine turned to him.

"Still having fun?"

"Actually, I'm more than ready to escape. Do I need permission?"

She laughed, the sound emitting a delightful gurgle from her exquisite throat. "You can't leave for at least another hal hour. Sorry. But I'll let you know the minute you're released from duty."

He groaned. "At least keep me company, then. That way we can joke later about the people we met."

"With pleasure," she replied sincerely. "Now, let's see Who was asking me to be introduced?"

It was much later when Nadine extricated him from a conversation with a bosomy women in a crimson dress.

"Okay, you've done your duty, Mr. Stebbing. At ease."

"Phew." Without delay he headed for the door. She gazed after him, a mixture of amusement and sadness in her eyes When he reached the door he looked around for her and saw she hadn't moved. He returned to her side.

"Aren't you coming?"

"Where?"

"With me. I want to be alone with you."

The words were ominous, but her desire to remain with him after the success of the evening was too strong to refuse She agreed to walk with him to his hotel. She said goodnigh to Everett, picked up her jacket from the office where she had left it, and met Lawrence in the entrance to the gallery. They took the elevator in silence. A cool breeze greeted them on the pavement, and Lawrence helped her into the beige jacke Charlotte had persuaded her to borrow. He maintained his hold on her hand when they started walking up Fifth Avenue.

"I'd like you to come up to my room for our own celebra tory nightcap." It was a statement, not a request.

If she went with him, wouldn't they inevitably make love At the rate her heart was pounding, at the weak feeling around her knees when he flashed his disarming smile at her at the yearning to feel his arms around her—she would not be able to stop him. She wouldn't want to stop him.

"No." It was a plea.

"Then we'll go to your apartment."

"No!" This time it was a cry.

His hand tightened on hers, and she sensed his frustration. "Why?" he asked after they'd walked a few blocks in silence. "Tell me why you're holding back. You know I'm crazy about you, and sometimes I get glimpses of the old Nadine who used to be crazy about me. Other times I get a snow queen who looks as if she's afraid she'll melt into nothingness if I touch her. What are you afraid of?"

She replied slowly, "I am afraid of melting."

"Then melt! Why deny yourself something that you'll enjoy?" When she didn't say anything he asked, "You still haven't forgiven me, have you? I've said I'm sorry in every way I know how, but you still can't forgive me."

"I've forgiven you," she protested. "That's not why I don't want to sleep with you again."

"Then what is it?"

"I don't want to go through what I went through last time. I couldn't make it through the separation again." Her voice trembled. "Neither of us has really changed, Lawrence. I'm still possessive and insecure and jealous, and you're still free-spirited and selfish. Right now you happen to be attracted to me—but for how long? You're returning to Florence; I'm staying in New York. What's the point of getting involved again?"

There was displeasure in his tone.

"You constantly surprise me, Nadine. Don't you see how much I care for you? You say you've forgiven me, but you don't trust me. Yet I'm sure you care for me too. You're not giving our feelings a chance to grow again."

"But don't you see, that's exactly it," she explained, feeling panicked by his chipping away at her wall of reserve. "Of course I care for you. But I don't want my feelings to be allowed to grow out of control so that I'll be—upset about your departure."

Lawrence seemed preoccupied.

"You see," she went on, thinking he didn't understand, "I

care for other things even more than I care for you."

His jaw tightened. "What, may I ask, are those othe things?"

"I've told you. Security, dependability. I won't fall in love with someone I can't rely on and trust."

"Do you imagine that spending the night with me wil precipitate your falling in love all over again?" he asked.

Fall in love with him all over again? Never. Never! Bu she didn't reply. She felt unsettled by the night—and by Lawrence. They had reached the Pierre Hotel and stood waiting, Lawrence's eyes searching her own.

"It's not even ten o'clock. Come on up for a short while a least."

Still she hesitated. She did not fool herself that she would only be going upstairs for a short while. She was torn with longing to be held by him, to spend the night in his arms rocked to sleep by the rhythm of their lovemaking, hearing whispered endearments, and waking to find his breath on he cheek, his eyes smiling into hers. Surely one night of plea sure to consummate the wonderful evening would not threaten her precarious emotions?

Without speaking she took his hand, and they turned and walked up the stairs to the brightly lit lobby. She caught sigh of herself in the large mirror that lined the yellow-gold mar ble walls and was amazed. Her cheeks were flushed, her gray eyes wide, and her walk had relaxed to an unaccustomed alluring sway. Lawrence spoke to the receptionist, then led her to the elevator.

When the bedroom door had closed behind them, Nadine slipped off the jacket and kicked off the white high heels then skipped in the cobwebby stockings to the window. She pushed it open. The tang in the autumn wind brushed against her closed eyelids. Even the thought of winter could not quel the excitement stirring in her breast. Maybe it won't be so cold this year, she was thinking. Maybe it won't be so lonely

Lawrence stood behind her and slipped his arms around her

waist. She leaned her head back against his shoulder and let her lids flutter half closed. She could just make out the yellow taxis and the horses and carriages winding their way along Fifty-ninth Street. Central Park was enveloped in darkness. For some reason she no longer feared the emotions Lawrence was raising in her. His lips brushed the top of her shiny hair. She sighed. His hands tightened and his thumbs stroked the undersides of her breasts. A knock on the door broke into her thoughts, too deep and wordless to be shared even with Lawrence.

While Lawrence accepted the silver ice bucket with champagne, Nadine stretched like a cat in the comfortable armchair. Just for one night, she thought dreamily, she would be someone else. She would not worry about the inevitable end to their affair, she would not think about commitment and security. She was not Nadine Barnet; she was someone else, a mysterious, lovely woman who had been chosen by the famous artist as his special companion for the evening. It might never happen again, and she was determined to enjoy it.

Lawrence took off his jacket and tie, then poured them champagne. While they drank they held hands and talked about the show.

"I've always loved your paintings," Nadine told him, seriously. "But I don't think I used to understand them. Remember I told you that your paintings were different now? I think maybe I'm the one who's changed, not your work. I understand it now in a way I couldn't before."

Lawrence replied after a silence, "I wish I could say I felt the same way about you. I've always loved you, but I still don't understand you. You've changed, and yet instead of knowing more, I know less. You were never so reserved! Here in New York I've seen a side of you I never imagined you possessing. You were always so outgoing, forthright—"

"I know, I know." She leaned over and put a finger to his lips. "Let's not talk about it right now."

He gently pulled her out of the chair and into his arms, folding her against his chest and bringing her mouth to his. At first his gentleness lulled her into a state of such sublime contentment she thought she could never pull herself out of it; soon, however, the kiss became demanding, urging, an argument of tongues and lips and teeth. Peace turned into excitement.

He broke away from her mouth and said almost harshly, "I made a mistake in thinking I could bring you up here for a cozy chat and nothing more. I can't seem to keep my hands off you, Nadine."

"I took that for granted," she replied, resting her smooth cheek against his, after giving him a warmly teasing smile.

"You're brighter than I am." He groaned in mock frustration before kissing her again. More gently he asked, "Are you sure you won't regret this tomorrow?"

She shook her head. "Not unless I get pregnant." Her eyes were closed, not meeting his.

There was a long silence. Nadine wondered if he had read more into her words than she meant. But at length he said softly, "We'll manage somehow. Will you trust me?"

She nodded, barely perceptibly, her hot cheek still on his. Lawrence rose and pulled her to her feet. They stood less than a foot apart, drinking in the other's expression. She was consumed with desire, but in the depth of that desire there was still a reserve. Lawrence unzipped the side of her dress and pulled it over the top of her head. She remained bravely where she was, in her filmy underwear and the thin, cobwebby stockings. His mouth brushed her throat, then, with lazy determination, found its way to her sculpted collarbone, down the sensitive breastbone, under one of her pale breasts, climbing slowly to its rosy peak. Her head fell back when he tugged this last gently between his teeth. She buried her hand in his thick hair and gave an unrestrained moan of excitement.

Straightening, Lawrence impatiently unbuttoned his shirt so that the soft weave of dark hair on his chest was exposed.

Nadine slipped over to the bedside lamp to turn it off. He stopped her, saying, "I haven't been able to look at you for too long." His voice was a mixture of humor and tenderness. "Don't turn it off."

They used to delight in making love with the light on, reveling in the visual planes and curves and colors of each other's flesh, excited by the other's expression of pleasure, exploring with unabashed wonder the mysteries and beauty of the human form. Could she lose herself to Lawrence with that same wild abandon he probably remembered in her? she wondered uneasily.

When he came over to her, shirtless, and penetrated her clear eyes with his own, she knew that he'd sensed her sudden tension. His long, tapered fingers gripped her shoulders.

"Can't you tell me what's wrong? You're acting more like a virgin than you did when you actually were one." His frustration frightened her, and he saw that it did. He loosened his grip, pushed a strand of her hair behind her ear caressingly. "You know I don't want to do this unless you want to." His faintly strangled tone belied this assertion: His arousal was more than evident when he pulled her gently to him again. After a moment he set her on the bed and carefully stripped her of the silk stockings and thin underpants. His mouth caressed her heels, her ankles, with ticklish sensuality. He had loved her feet—slim, high-arched, long-toed—and had often devoured them with kisses while they talked away the night hours. He stretched himself on the bed at last, alongside her, and she reached over to unzip his trousers.

But his hand closed over hers, stopping her.

"Sweetheart, look at me."

She couldn't obey. The hand, still enclosing hers, moved to her chin and nudged her face toward his. He went on, "You may still want to keep your secret, and you may not want to tell me why you're tense and afraid, and I haven't pressed you too much to tell me. But look at this from my position for a moment. I want you. I've done everything I know to try to get close to you. You won't let me. Now I can't tell if you're willing to make love just for my sake, or for Everett's sake, or for some mysterious reason that I haven't a clue about. I don't like not knowing."

"There's no mysterious reason," she replied. "Just this one." She guided his hand to the site of her body's testament to its sweet excitement.

"That's not exactly what I meant," he pursued, caressing her with delicious slowness. She closed her eyes. "Although I'm glad you want me as much as I want you. But I'm still confused. I feel shut out. What happened when you came back to New York after you left me? What is this thing about you that Everett knows and I don't? I want you to tell me."

She shook her head faintly. Not now, she was thinking. We can't spoil everything now. She had to be sure. Absolutely sure he wouldn't take Jamie from her. Her body was growing increasingly delirious under his gently exploring fingers.

"Did you meet someone else? Were you badly hurt again?"

Another faint shake of her head. "No one else, Lawrence." Her hips strained from the bed as she was brought precariously close to the dizzying height of ecstasy. He lightened his touch. His low voice sounded amazed.

"No other man for four years, Nadine? With a body like yours and responses like yours? I find that very hard to believe."

There was a barely perceptible shrug. She did not care whether or not he believed her; she wished he would stop talking and let her revel in the astounding sensations his hand created in her. But he was persistent.

"Why not?"

He had reached her at last. His caresses had worn thin her reserve; his familiar smell, his quiet, persistent voice, brought back shudderingly exquisite memories of closeness, of superb tenderness and understanding. But she didn't want to regain that closeness, as he wanted to. She felt too fragile to leave herself vulnerable to another heartbreak. So she flared up, her gray eyes opening with a dark flash, her face flushed with the heated pulse that throbbed under her skin.

"You know why not." She pushed the words out of her mouth rapidly, as though they burned. "Who are you to pry me with questions like these, to want me to be someone I no longer am? Why should I confide in you? You broke my heart once—why should I trust you with it again? What have you done to make me think I could trust you again? We're both adults, we both know what we want right now. Sex. Pure and simple. But you're not satisfied with just my body! No, you want to possess my heart and soul as well, God knows why. But you can't have those; I'm keeping them where they'll be safe. You can have me—we can have each other—but you can't hurt me again."

Lawrence had pulled himself up against the mountains of white pillows, his hands clasped behind his head, eyeing her with an infuriating expression of lazy appreciation. Nadine swung her slim legs over the side of the bed, but he reached out and pulled her back to his side.

"We'll forget it then," he replied easily to the angry questioning look she threw him. "I can wait a little longer, but I'm certainly not going to leave myself open to a later accusation that I only wanted to have sex with you. Besides, it wouldn't be enough for me. Sorry, Nadine. You'll just have to wait too."

She pulled herself upright and glared at him. Her bare chest heaved.

"If you're doing this to punish me . . ."

He made no movement.

"I'm not punishing you. I simply don't want to make love until you want to. Really want to, I mean, not just have sex to relieve your four years of abstinence. Maybe I'm selfish and arrogant to want my love for you returned, but it sure would be nicer than your even more selfish demand for mere sexual gratification."

"Your love returned!" she spat back at him. "You don't even know what the word means!"

He seemed determined not to get angry. Mildly, he replied, "If your definition of love is the jealous hysteria it was four years ago, then maybe you're right."

She stood up, blistering.

"Where are you going?" he asked politely.

"You've humiliated me and insulted me." Her voice shook with rage. "I'm going home."

"It's the other way around. You've humiliated and insulted me." Lawrence was maddeningly calm. "You deceived me by letting me think you cared for me enough to sleep with me when you really didn't give a damn in hell about anything except your personal gratification. And you insulted me by assuming I'd be willing just to have sex with you, without any of the 'making love' part."

"You teased me—led me on—" She picked up her white gauzy dress and clenched it in two fists in front of her.

"My dear girl, don't imagine I'm any less aroused than you," he returned implacably. "I just have a little more pride."

"Pride!" Her eyes glittered.

He rolled over and swung his bare feet onto the carpet. His expression was enigmatic as he walked toward her.

"Yes, sweetheart. Pride. Too much of it to 'have sex' with the woman I love after she has stressed the fact that she feels nothing for me." He reached out and one by one removed her clenched fingers from the dress, then draped it over the back of the crimson armchair. There was a trace of weariness in his voice as he said, "If you'd told me you were in love with me, and I responded—furiously, mind—that under no circumstances could I ever love you, but I demanded that you gratefully accept the 'pure and simple sex' I offered, don't tell me you'd go ahead."

She was forced to silence.

"Good. Now you understand my view, even if I don't

understand yours. Sex without love, marriage without love . . ." He eyed her with a mixture of resignation and amazement. "For what purpose, Nadine?"

She said slowly, looking at the dress on the chair but not putting it on, "You should understand that. After all, you had sex with Lily but you told me you were in love with me. That was sex without love, or did you love us both?"

He said with a sigh, "That was four years ago. My values were different then. What happened to *your* decision not to sleep with anyone without a prior commitment from him? Have you changed your mind about that?"

Just for one night, she wanted to cry out, I tried to be someone else, someone without nagging worries and brooding memories. But Lawrence had not allowed her to be anyone but herself.

"No," she replied, still slowly. "I just forgot about it temporarily. Another lapse."

The tiredness crept back into his voice. "I happen to know how much easier it is to just have sex with someone you're not in love with. It's impossible with someone you're in love with, if she's not in love with you. So I do understand why you're more willing than I."

He sounded sincere; he sounded sad.

"I'm sorry, Lawrence." Her voice was sad too. She was sorry he had broken her heart irreparably, she was sorry she no longer loved him. It was too late now; she had changed too much.

He ran a hand abstractly through his thick hair and gave her another touching smile.

"Don't leave," he asked. "Making love is only one part of what I long to do with you. Talking's another. Sleeping together . . ." He regarded her frankly. "You'll stay, won't you?"

To her own surprise, she agreed after a moment's hesitation. It was partly her feeling of compassion for him, partly her reluctance to return to her lonely apartment, or to sleep on the couch at her sister's where Jamie was. She'd have to wake up early to take Jamie to school; she'd think up an excuse in the morning.

"Don't get dressed," he said, when she reached for the dress again. "I'll turn out the light and we'll talk in the dark."

"I'm cold, though." It was true. Goose bumps covered her body from the fall wind blowing in the open window. Lawrence strode over to the closet and took a fresh blue cotton shirt from its hanger.

"Wear this. You'll be more comfortable."

She put it on. It fell halfway down her thighs, and she buttoned it demurely to her chest. Lawrence took off his trousers and underpants and walked unself-consciously to the bed. He reached for the lamp.

Nadine made her way to his side in the dark.

"Come here," he said when she sat uncertainly on the edge of the bed. "I'll warm you up." He crooked one arm around her and rubbed her back and shoulders with the other as she half turned and rested her cheek on his broad chest. She felt comforted.

Now was the moment to tell him about Jamie. She stared into the dark room, feeling closer to him than she had in a long while. Before he came to Charlotte's tomorrow, before he found out some other way, he should learn about his son.

She cleared her throat.

"Lawrence?"

Silence.

"Lawrence?"

A gentle snore was her only response. A combination of relief and annoyance filled her. Knowing he was asleep, she allowed her hand to caress the soft mat of hair on his chest, and his firm stomach. He stirred slightly in his sleep as she slipped her hand to his lower abdomen, but he did not wake up. Eventually she too drifted off to sleep, mingled anxiety and contentment making her dream restlessly and exhaustedly.

Chapter Nine

Anxiety overtook the fleeting joy of being held in Lawrence's arms the night before. Nervously awaiting Lawrence's arrival, Nadine helped Charlotte clean up after the children's early supper. Billy and Cory had disappeared into the den to watch a western on television. Jamie, however, refused to leave his mother's side. With the unerring instincts of a four-year-old, he sensed that in some way he was troublesome to her that night and as a consequence pestered her for more attention than usual.

The sound of crashing glass made her jump in alarm.

"Jamie, be careful!" she cried. He had dropped a full glass of water on the floor.

"It's all right," Charlotte broke in hastily, seeing Jamie's hurt look at Nadine's snappiness. "Let me sweep up those pieces. Careful, Jamie. Let me do it. We don't want you cutting yourself."

But Jamie, ashamed, wanted to help clear away the pieces. Suddenly he issued a loud wail and held up his finger. A trickle of blood wended its way down it.

"Oh, Jamie!" Nadine was cross and worried.

At her increased annoyance, Jamie wailed louder.

"Hush, now hush," Charlotte urged him, seeing Nadine about to burst into tears herself or break into anger. "Nadine, go into the living room, will you, and pour yourself a drink? I know Steve would like company. I'll put a Band-Aid on Jamie's finger and put him to bed. It's past time, anyway.''

"No!" Jamie wailed. "No! I want to stay with Mommy!"

Nadine's anxious heart melted at the sight of his sad, fierce expression.

"I'm not going anywhere," she soothed him. "Come along with me, and I'll fix your finger up. We'll leave Auntie Charlotte to clean up the kitchen. Come on, sweetheart."

She picked him up in her strong arms and with an apologetic smile to her sister took him down the hallway to the guest room where he slept. In the adjoining bathroom she bathed and dressed his minor cut, talking to him, calming him, then she tenderly undressed him and tucked him into bed.

Jamie's dark green eyes stared after her when the door closed with an expression of sadness and defiance.

In the living room Steve glanced up from the *New York Times* and gave her a cheerful smile.

"Drink, old thing? You look like you need one."

"I suppose I do. A scotch would be nice."

"One scotch coming up." Steve went over to the well-stocked bar. "Don't you think you should reconsider telling your friend he has a son? It's driving you crazy, trying to keep the blasted secret, and Jamie's sensitive enough to be affected by your worrying. Lawrence sounds like a nice guy—"

"Steve, please!" Nadine's anxiety pressed in on her again. "We've been over this before. I can't risk Jamie's fate on the chance that Lawrence won't try to take him from me."

Seeing her tortured look, Steve amiably dropped the subject. Nadine was about to return to Charlotte in the kitchen, when the doorbell rang. Her heart pounded in her throat. Steve's kind brown eyes smiled at her.

"Courage, old girl," he admonished. "We're here to protect you! I'll warn him when I let him in."

"Thanks," she teased back, but her gray eyes still looked

worried. Steve disappeared down the hall. Hastily, she sat on a plush blue chair trying to look relaxed, then, when she heard voices, jumped up again and stood in front of the window.

"Hi, Lawrence," she greeted him when he entered the room.

"Hi, Nadine." His greeting was cool, his eyes warm. He wore a dark green shetland sweater over a paler cotton shirt, and black, straight-legged pants. Blushing, she allowed him to brush her lips with his before he accepted Steve's offer of a drink.

Over dinner the tension that had settled in the apartment before Lawrence's arrival evaporated completely. Even Nadine's calm gray eyes sparkled mischievously, and she joined in the lively discourse on Italian versus American life-styles without constraint. The meal was excellent: thin filets of steak cooked in red wine sauce and served with two excellent bottles of California wine were topped off with a scrumptious dessert of chocolate mousse and a large bowl of fruit.

Coffee was served in the living room, and the conversation continued to flow without interruption. Charlotte filled Lawrence's cup with black coffee and handed him a platter of thin mint chocolates. She and Steve took the two armchairs on either side, maneuvering so that Nadine was forced to sit with Lawrence on the sofa. Lawrence offered the plate of chocolates to Nadine with a smile of such tenderness that she felt herself blush, and could barely thank him. It seemed so right, so wonderful, to be sitting beside him like this, she was thinking. Could she trust him? Could she?

A loud wail from behind the closed bedroom door down the hall almost made her drop her cup.

"Mommy!"

Hardly realizing what she was doing, Nadine set her cup on the table and was halfway to her feet when she found Lawrence's very surprised eyes on her. She subsided back onto the couch, wracked with worry, and looked with mute appeal at her sister. Trying to cover up the awful moment, Charlotte muttered a hasty excuse and hurried out of the room.

The others were left in uncomfortable silence. Steve stared at the floor, then roused himself to offer more coffee to his guests. Lawrence refused. Nadine accepted. Her hand shook too much to hold the cup steady, and Steve took it from her. He gave her a look pregnant with meaning, but she did not acknowledge it.

Jamie's cries grew louder. "Mommy! I want Mommy."

Nadine's misery swelled. She could not let Jamie cry without responding. Why, oh, why had she ever agreed to this wretched, disastrous evening?

Lawrence's voice reached her, expressionlessly.

"You'd better go, don't you think?"

She should have told him right away, she realized too late, miserably getting to her feet and leaving the room.

She took Jamie from her sister, and his wails ceased almost immediately, although he continued to sob quietly.

"He'll be okay," Nadine told Charlotte. "You can go back."

Seeing the despair in her eyes, Charlotte gave her sister a hug in the dark room. "It's best that it happened," she said sympathetically. "It's not fair to keep it a secret. You'd hate it too, if it were the other way around."

Nadine did not reply.

The door closed softly behind her sister, and Jamie clung to Nadine, gulping back his sobs. Automatically Nadine whispered soothing words and gentle murmurs of endearment, her mind dreading her inevitable return to the living room, where she would have to face Lawrence's quizzical, angry eyes again. But Charlotte was right. She deserved his anger: If he had kept a secret like this she would have been furious too.

She heard the door open behind her and glanced around. Lawrence stood in the dim light, staring at his son. Jamie lifted his head from his mother's shoulder and gazed back curiously. Nadine did nothing to break the moment.

"Hello, Jamie." Lawrence's voice was soft.

Nadine's clung more tightly to her son.

"Hello," Jamie mumbled back, his eyes wide.

Lawrence walked toward them, his eyes still fastened on Jamie.

"You should have told me," he said.

Nadine shook her head, her throat constricted. She lowered Jamie back onto the bed and tucked the blankets around him. Jamie remained silent, not taking his eyes off his father. The parents looked down at the small boy curled up in the bed, then Nadine muttered with difficulty: "We can't talk here."

"Maybe not here," he agreed, still not looking at her. "But we're going to talk."

Gently he leaned over and kissed the side of Jamie's head. As if by magic, Jamie was already asleep. Quietly Nadine left the room, and Lawrence followed.

In the dimly lit corridor Lawrence asked:

"Were you planning on leaving Jamie with your sister overnight? I presume he stayed here last night too?"

"Yes." Nadine's voice was small.

Charlotte and Steve regarded them apprehensively when they entered. Lawrence said curtly, "Nadine tells me it's all right for her to leave Jamie with you overnight. I hope you don't mind—we have some talking to do."

Neither Charlotte nor Steve made any objection. "It was a pleasure meeting you," Steve said. "I hope we'll see you again."

Charlotte sensed Lawrence's anger, and now her sympathy was all for her sister. She put an arm around her as they walked toward the front door. Lawrence kept up a facade of conventional thanks and appreciation to his hosts, shook their hands, and headed for the stairwell, not bothering to wait for the elevator. Breathless and a little scared, Nadine followed him down the marble steps to the lobby.

An autumn chill in the air made her shiver. Ignoring her, Lawrence looked down the street for a taxi.

"Where are we going?" she asked, not sure if she was trembling most from nervousness or from cold.

His voice made her colder still.

"Since now I understand why you haven't invited me to your apartment before, maybe we can go there. Unless you have any more secrets?"

She did not reply. He hailed a cab and held the door open for her. Nadine gave her address to the driver.

They did not speak a word the entire way. Nadine stared straight ahead, trying to keep up her courage. She could sense fury rising in Lawrence, and remembering her past brushes with his temper, she grew increasingly unhappy.

She should not be ashamed of her apartment, she told herself, for although it was small, it was comfortable and homey. Jamie's room was tidy, the kitchen clean, and the living room cozy. But tonight, with Lawrence in a silent, towering rage beside her, the apartment seemed cramped and ugly. She wondered if he was angry at the thought of his son being brought up in a place like this when he could be roaming the fresh green hills of Fiesole. It was impossible to read his expression.

"Do you want coffee or a drink?" she suggested nervously.

He did not bother replying.

"You should have told me," he repeated. His voice shook with anger.

"I meant to tell you," she replied, trying to keep her voice even. "I didn't want him to be exposed to all the publicity you were getting. I wanted to wait till after the show. Then last night I meant to tell you—"

He interrupted harshly. "I don't mean last night, or last week, either. I mean four years ago. Did you know when you left me? When you were sick at the train station?"

"No."

"When did you find out?"

"January."

"You should have told me then."

Nadine braced herself for battle. She folded her arms.

"What should I have told you? Jamie is mine. Only mine."

"Steve told me how old Jamie is, and I'm perfectly capable of doing arithmetic. I'm also fairly well informed in the appropriate biology. As far as I know it is quite impossible for any child to be 'only' a woman's."

His scathing sarcasm made her wince, but she lifted her chin.

"You know perfectly well what I mean."

"No, I don't." Lawrence raised his voice. "I don't have the least idea what you mean. You should have told me! I could at least have helped you financially, even if you never wanted to see me again."

"I've managed perfectly well on my own. I didn't want your help and I didn't need it."

His eyes darkened. "Steve said you were borrowing money from him until just over two years ago."

"What if I was?" she flashed back. "I've paid him back. Besides, aren't you glad your son wasn't brought up in the lap of luxury, as I was? Remember how contemptuous you were of my spoiled upbringing? Aren't you glad I've finally learned the true value of money? Aren't you glad I had to struggle, and aren't you glad your son had the opportunity to be included in the struggle? You always thought so highly of yourself for having suffered poverty and bastardy—aren't you grateful your son has had the same enriching upbringing?"

He said very coldly, "I was never contemptuous of you, Nadine. And I would never allow a child of mine to endure the poverty I endured as a child if I could help it."

Resentfully, she replied, "I'm not bringing up *my* child in poverty. We're managing quite well."

With an effort, Lawrence held on to his temper. "You're

not managing well enough. You're not just denying *your* child his father but you're denying *my* child his mother. You have to work, you have to leave him most of the day. If you liked your job I'd understand it, but you don't even like what you're doing!''

She regarded him levelly. His anger, his logic, his controlled fury, infuriated her. It was all so familiar that they could have been back in the villa four years ago, saying things that could never be forgiven or forgotten. Once again, she had opened herself to this man, and given him the power to wound her.

''I'm not denying Jamie anything, Lawrence. Nothing. He has a mother who is with him as much as possible, and he has relatives who take extremely good care of him at other times. You have no right to criticize what I've done or how I've done it. I've done the best I could.''

''It wasn't the best you could do, and you know it.'' Lawrence started pacing up and down the small kitchen area. ''You denied me my child, and consequently denied yourself the means to bring him up in some security.''

''Sorry, Lawrence. But I didn't deny you anything. You denied him. You didn't want to take any kind of responsibility for the relationship between us, much less any kind of commitment. You didn't want to be saddled with me; you certainly didn't want to be saddled with a child. You think that you're a man of honor because you married Lily when she said she was pregnant; do you think I would have wanted to marry you for a reason like that? Do you think love is the same as honor? I fell in love with you, and I was willing to accept the relationship on your terms because of that. I didn't leave you because you went off with Lily; I left you because you abused the freedom and lack of commitment in our relationship. That's when you lost any right you had to your child.''

''If I'd known about Jamie,'' he replied through clenched teeth, ''I might have felt differently.''

"You mean you would have married me because I was having your child?" Nadine was sarcastic. "Come on, Lawrence, do you really think I'd be happy marrying you because of Jamie? You must know by now that I'm more selfish and possessive than that! I wanted your love, not your damned feeling of obligation!"

Lawrence swung around and stood directly in front of her. She flinched but met his gaze steadily.

"That's right," he said angrily. "That's nearer the point. Your pride was hurt, and you wanted to punish me. You think you lost your lousy pride by falling in love with me, and you refused to ask for my help. You were punishing me not only by denying me my child and denying me the opportunity to help you both, but by denying my own feelings about you. That's the real reason you wrote that sickening letter."

Nadine's eyes were black with bitterness.

"Feelings!" she exclaimed scathingly. "Don't tell me you have those?"

Lawrence's jaw tightened. He shoved his hands in his pockets and stood rigidly before her.

"Don't be sarcastic, Nadine Barnet. You know as well as I do that I fell as deeply in love with you as you did with me. You know as well as I do that you were just as difficult to live with as I was. Don't put all the guilt for our separation on my shoulders. You were the one who wasn't honest with herself in the beginning. You were the one who said she wanted independence, when you didn't even know what the word meant. You were the one who started whining and moping and accusing, unjustly, I might add. And you were the one who finally left me. I didn't leave you. In spite of all your tantrums I loved you. I loved you so much I put aside any pride I lost when you walked out on me to write to you. Not once, but twice, even after a letter like the one you sent me. For God's sake, get down off your pedestal and face up to the facts: I'm not a blackguard; I'm not a cheat; I'm not a traitor. And take me off the pedestal you put me on, while you're at it. I'm not and I never was the ideal, perfect, virtuous man you imagined me to be. I'm just a guy who's in love with you."

Nadine felt her heart contract. If only that were true! But how could she believe him now? She willed the growing surge of emotion to subside.

"Was in love, you mean," she corrected.

"Unlike you," he replied coldly, "I say what I mean. I am in love with you."

She turned her back and walked over to the fireplace in the living room. "You may be infatuated," she said slowly. "You probably do get infatuated with the women you have sex with, and maybe you call it love in order to ease your conscience about screwing around, but that's not what I call love. As soon as you get tired of making love to me, as soon as some problem arises that you don't want to bother with, you'll find another woman. Infatuation doesn't give you the right to criticize how I bring up my child."

"And I suppose in your mind selfishness, jealousy, and possessiveness are equated with love, is that it? What kind of love was it that made you walk out on me? What kind of love was it that made you write that letter?"

The small, dingy room was white-hot now with the bitterness and resentment pent up for four years. Sharp accusations and harsh words were hurled through the tense atmosphere, striking with blows as fast and sharp as physical ones. Grimly, they retaliated with reminders of other wounds, of times of treachery and unfaithfulness and faithlessness. Finally Lawrence exploded, shouting angrily:

"Dammit, that was years ago! How can you harp on things that don't matter any longer? I've changed, and you've changed! It's our relationship now that I'm concerned with: yours and mine and Jamie's."

"You always did have a gift for being able to sweep under the rug anything that made you uncomfortable," she screamed back at him. "What you don't realize is that what happened four years ago has a very important bearing on what's happening right now. Yes, you're right: I've changed. You taught me how, and I learned my lesson like the good little schoolgirl you thought I was. You're damned right I've changed!"

"What did I teach you?"

"To never trust you again. Never." Her voice was charged with finality, with a bitter memory of the deep hurt he had bestowed on her years ago.

His jaw tightened in angry passion, and the tips of his thin nostrils whitened. He walked over to her and gave his head a slight shake as though to clear the red-hot coals which glowed in his brain.

For a moment Nadine was afraid Lawrence would strike her. Her gray-black eyes flashed defiantly, and she tilted her chin proudly, daring him to do so.

He did not strike her, but his next words were worse than any physical blow.

"You're a fool, Nadine. Jamie's my son too. I won't allow my son to grow up without a father and with only half a mother."

Her almond-shaped eyes widened; hollow fear took the place of defiance. This was what she had feared above all: that he would take Jamie from her!

"Don't you dare!" she spat out, her voice icy with venom. "I'll never let Jamie go! I'll never let you do to him what you did to me. I got over your betrayal—barely. A child would be scarred for life if you deserted him. I'll never let you back into my life or into Jamie's either! Never, Lawrence!"

"I never betrayed you," he protested again. "I'll never betray Jamie. Will you stop this melodrama?"

Nadine gulped at her raging fear, swallowing it like burning liquid. No matter what it took, she would fight him. She would protect what she had: her pride, her security, and her son.

"I'm not going to argue semantics with you," she said, trying to inject scorn in her voice to disguise the fear. "I won't let you hurt my son as you hurt me. I can't forgive you for his sake, if not for my own."

There was a brief silence. They heard an ambulance scream its way up Broadway; someone trudged up the narrow wooden stairs outside. Their eyes were locked, unmoving.

"I was wrong." Lawrence finally broke the silence. "You haven't changed one bit. You're still the same jealous, possessive, immature little girl I used to know, and now it looks as if you'll never grow up to be a woman."

He turned and stalked out of the small apartment, slamming the heavy door behind him.

You haven't changed either, Nadine thought, staring at the painted black door. You always had a knack for walking out in the middle of an argument.

Chapter Ten

After a sleepless night, Nadine awoke early and fixed herself coffee, wishing Jamie were there to keep her company and distract her from the fear that Lawrence might simply kidnap the child and take him to Florence. Would Lawrence stoop so low? Surely he would fight fairly for custody of the child.

While the water boiled for coffee, Nadine went into the tiny bathroom to wash. Dark purple smudges under her eyes made her fair skin seem even paler. She slipped into a warm navy wool dress, brushed her hair until tears stung her eyes, then gulped her coffee quickly and set off for work. It was a bleak, gray October day, and threatening, heavy clouds lowered over the tops of Manhattan's skyscrapers. Because she was early she decided to walk through the park to her office.

How had they allowed themselves to fight all over again last night? she wondered sadly. She had begun to hope that they had changed enough to start over. In the back of her mind, in fact, she had had flitting imaginings of the three of them all together, her anxiety for her son, her endless working hours, her loneliness all over for ever. If only she and Lawrence had had more time getting to know each other again, a confidence might have built up between them. She would have told him about Jamie, and they could have discussed the situation rationally and with sympathetic understanding. But to learn about Jamie's existence by accident must have appalled him; and her own fear that he would try to take Jamie from her had added fuel to the fire.

Downhearted, Nadine turned a narrow path toward the pond and felt a few heavy drops of rain on her head. She had left her umbrella behind. Sighing, she wondered whether she should call Lawrence and apologize for her part of the fight, then wondered if he had left New York already, without saying goodbye. What did he think of her? "Jealous, possessive, and immature." It was inconceivable that he would want to speak to her again. It was amazing that he ever had in the first place. Nadine's self-confidence dwindled still lower as the rain grew heavier.

Luckily it was a busy morning and she did not have much time to dwell on her thoughts. Before she took her lunch break she decided to call Lawrence that afternoon and see if he had left for Florence yet. If he had not she would give him the apology she owed him.

The phone rang at her desk, and she picked up the receiver.

"Mills Gallery. Nadine Barnet speaking."

"Nadine, it's Lawrence." He sounded contrite. "I'm sorry I walked out like that. It was a stupid thing to do."

She was at a loss for words. She hadn't expected him to telephone at all, much less to apologize for walking out on her. He made it sound as though that was the hardest thing to forgive, and it made the rest of their shouting match seem less important by comparison.

"That's okay," she said softly. "I guess you were pretty mad by then."

"We didn't resolve anything," Lawrence continued. "Will you invite me over for dinner tonight so we can finish our discussion in a more civilized manner? I promise not to walk out, and I'll try not to get mad. I think I was angry enough last night to last me a whole year in any case."

Nadine gave a small, relieved laugh. "I'd like that. The problem is that Jamie will be there, and I don't want to fight in front of him."

Lawrence replied, "We won't fight. We'll just talk."

"Really?" She was dubious.

"Really," he assured her, a smile in his voice. "Why don't I drop by your sister's and bring Jamie to your place in a cab?"

Nadine hesitated. "I can pick him up."

"But it's no bother for me. I'd like to talk to him alone." There was a wistfulness in his tone that melted Nadine's heart. It was absurd that she had imagined Lawrence might abduct the child.

"All right," she agreed. "It would be more convenient."

The relief in Lawrence's voice was evident, and Nadine felt another pang. "Don't bother to shop; Jamie and I will pick up some Chinese take-out. What time will you be home?"

"Five-thirtyish."

"See you then."

He was gone. Suddenly the dark sky outside her office window seemed not quite so dark anymore, and the thick stack of memorandums from Everett seemed not quite so tedious. With a lightened heart she attacked the first one vigorously.

She left work at three, pleading a headache to Everett, and treated herself to a cab uptown, stopping at the little grocery store on the street corner for some candles, coffee, and a log for the fireplace. Inside her apartment she looked around critically. It was indeed dark and shabby, she thought, remembering with hot cheeks Lawrence's accusations of the previous evening. Still, she could tidy it up to give the impression of coziness and comfort at least. It did not take long to plump the cheerfully colored cushions on the worn sofa, and she tossed a bright red-and-orange shawl on the back of the green armchair, covering the dark stain on its back. She took out a red-and-white-checked tablecloth that she rarely used and spread it on the kitchen table, and lit two tall candles on it. She put another candle on the low coffee table in front of the fire, then she switched on the soft lamp by the wide bed in the far corner so that the room was lit in a warm glow. The green curtains were drawn against the deepening dusk outside. Satisfied, she changed into warm gray corduroy pants and a soft red sweater that clung to her slim figure, then lay down on the couch with a book to await their arrival.

They came up the stairs hand in hand, and Nadine watched from her front door, a queer feeling of delight and envy in her breast as she saw Jamie's look of adoration—usually reserved for her alone—fixed on Lawrence. A large brown shopping bag was cradled in Lawrence's other arm. He threw Nadine a quizzical look and kissed her cheek affectionately. To her surprise she felt her cheeks flame and tried to hide the blush by reaching down and hugging Jamie. He said excitedly:

"Lawrence wants to see my drawings, Mommy! I showed him the one we did at school and he liked it."

"That's wonderful, darling." She smiled. "Then maybe Lawrence will show you some of his drawings too. Would you like that?"

Jamie's green eyes grew round. "Do you draw too?" he asked Lawrence, awed.

"As a matter of fact, yes, I do."

Jamie was impressed. "I didn't know that grown-ups could draw. Mrs. Smith can't." He led the way into the living room.

Lawrence and Nadine shared another look, one of pride and tenderness this time, and she blushed again. She should hate this man who had threatened to take her child away, but she couldn't stop her heart from racing when she saw him.

"Hey, this looks wonderful!" Lawrence murmured, glancing into the living-room area. "What'd you do? Take off from work today?"

"It wasn't that bad last night, was it?" Nadine teased.

He set the bag of groceries on the kitchen table and took off his wet raincoat. "It must've been my imagination, then." He glanced around at the cheerful fire in the hearth, the glowing candles, the comfortable-looking furniture.

He gave her a warm smile. "I brought some wine. Want to start with that? We'll heat up the Chinese food we brought."

Nadine took the containers from the bag. "There's enough here for a family of eight," she said, examining the boxes of egg rolls, cartons of soup, assorted spicy and mild main dishes, vegetable dishes, and rice.

"We'll save it for when we have more children if we can't finish it," Lawrence said wickedly, and when her startled eyes flew to his, he winked. "Where's your corkscrew?"

Nadine found it for him, and Jamie returned with several pads in his small arms.

"Why don't you take Lawrence over by the fire," Nadine suggested to him. "You can turn on the overhead light so that he can see your drawings better. I'll put some of this food in the oven. You guys must be starving if you think you'll be able to eat half this much."

Jamie agreed happily, and waited impatiently for Lawrence to finish uncorking the wine and to pour a glass for himself and Nadine. Then he tugged his trouser leg and took him to the sofa. In a moment the two heads were bent over the child's drawing pads, lost in conversation. Nadine gave a sigh, feeling excluded, but happy also for the respite to be able to pull her emotions together and let the happiness she felt at being with Lawrence again well up inside her. She might as well enjoy it now, she reminded herself, because in a couple of hours after they started talking he might very well stalk out into the rain again.

But her feeling of tranquillity only increased over dinner. Several times Lawrence threw back his head and laughed deeply in a way she remembered from their time together in Florence. She was touched too by Jamie's attempts to imitate his father's way of laughing, crinkling up his small eyes and putting his head back also. The conversation revolved mostly around the small boy, who confided to Lawrence about the teachers at his kindergarten. None of them liked his drawings, he told him, sadness fleeting across his brow for a split second. Lawrence seemed to know just what Jamie felt, because he didn't bother with hypocritical reassurances. Instead, he explained that an artist's work did not have to be liked.

"Some drawings are great simply because they aren't liked, Jamie," he went on, much to Nadine's surprise. She felt certain that Jamie couldn't possibly understand the concept Lawrence was trying to put across. But Jamie, his eyes fastened on Lawrence, seemed to listen intently. "Some drawings make people uncomfortable or angry or sad, but that doesn't mean they aren't good."

Jamie narrowed his eyes thoughtfully. "Yes," he replied finally. "I'm going to make drawings that make Mrs. Smith cross and uncomfy and they'll be good."

Both Nadine and Lawrence broke into laughter at Jamie's summation of Lawrence's mini-lecture, but Nadine was sure that part of his explanation had filtered into Jamie's unconscious and would help him to deal with school. Lawrence refilled her glass, and, unable to eat anything more, Nadine tipped her chair back, her almond eyes softened in the candlelight. She glanced at Lawrence. Impulsively he lifted his glass to hers.

"Here's to us," he said, smiling at her. "Here's to you and Jamie and me."

Jamie lifted his glass of milk too.

When even Jamie confessed he could not eat another thing, Nadine saw with surprise that it was way past his bedtime.

"No dishes tonight," she said, tossing the empty cartons into the trash. "You can pop off to bed now. Do you want coffee, Lawrence? I'll put the water on if you do."

He nodded, rising. "Is putting Jamie to bed an elaborate ritual?" he asked, going over to her. "If it isn't, do you think I can handle it tonight?"

Again Nadine hesitated. She had mixed feelings about the intimacy that was developing between Jamie and Lawrence. She was glad for Jamie's sake that he was getting to know his father, even if it was only for a few days, but she was not sure how Jamie would feel once Lawrence left, were he to grow too fond of him.

"All right," she said at last. Then she tried to ease over the intimate moment. "Jamie can probably teach you a thing or two about how to go to bed, so I'll let him show you what's to be done."

Lawrence gave another laugh, then bent his head and brushed her bare throat with his lips.

"You're looking lovely tonight," he murmured.

A shiver ran through Nadine, and she closed her eyes, lost in the tender moment. She could not help responding to his touch: One hand crept onto his shoulder, her face turned slightly, then their lips met. Lawrence spoke huskily:

"I'd like to tell him tonight."

She stiffened. "That you're his father?"

"Yes."

The kiss died on her lips, and she turned away to fill the coffee pot. But his touch had sent her thoughts into a jumble of confusion. She could not think of a good reason why Jamie should not know. She did not reply, and when she turned around to clear off the rest of the paper plates from the table, Lawrence and Jamie had left the room.

While the coffee was brewing, she took the rest of her wine to the living-room area and sat on the couch, staring thoughtfully into the fire. Lawrence—Jamie—and she. Jamie—she—and Lawrence. Her thoughts went around in circles, unable to spin out of that little web, as though she were in a trance. She—Lawrence—and Jamie. What good would be gained from telling Jamie that Lawrence was his father? He wasn't even four, after all. But on the other hand, what good would come of not telling him? She had always intended to tell him, when he was old enough. Maybe not the entire story of their passionate affair, but the circumstances surrounding it.

Lawrence stood in the doorway and she realized with a start that he had been standing there for a while. She raised her eyebrows questioningly, and he sat beside her on the couch.

"I think he was happy to know," Lawrence answered her unspoken question quietly. "He didn't seem surprised at all."

That was something she herself had considered. Father and son had recognized each other in a way that went beyond the boundary of a shared interest in drawing. They were kindred spirits in a very deep way. Nadine sipped her wine thoughtfully.

"What are we going to do?" she said at last. "Why all this friendliness and fatherliness? I don't understand it."

Lawrence replied seriously, "I'm trying to make friends with you, and since your life is wrapped up in Jamie, I'd like to make friends with him too. You know I didn't mean what I said last night. I'm not going to try to take him from you. Truly, Nadine, you're the one who matters to me."

She concentrated on the wineglass. You're falling for him, straight off the bell tower, and you're going to land hard on the pavement again, you foolish girl, an inner warning spoke to her. She said slowly, "It doesn't make any difference, though. We live separate lives, in separate countries. How often could we see each other; how often do you expect to see Jamie? It's futile for us to get involved again."

Lawrence shifted his position so that he was facing her and took her free hand in his. "At the moment that's true," he agreed. "But we can change that."

"How?"

"You could marry me."

Her hand escaped his, and she sat rigidly on the couch.

"That's impossible."

"Forget for a moment about our past relationship and all our problems and resentments. Look at it from a purely practical point of view. You could give up the job at the gallery, where you aren't happy, and could concentrate on finishing your master's thesis. You and Jamie could leave the city and move to Florence. He could be brought up in fresh air, beautiful countryside, great cultural surroundings, and with both his parents. And I would be living with the woman I love, my inspiration, my muse, and my family.''

At his words, Nadine gave a wry smile.

''That's okay from a romantic point of view. But what about all the other stuff? Think how I'd feel uprooted from everything I've built up over the past four years. I may dislike my job, and I may hate being in New York with Jamie, but at least it's security. At least I have an apartment and an income, and after what I've been through simply in order to get it, I can tell you I'd rather not risk giving it up.''

To her surprise, he did not get angry. ''I can understand that,'' he said. ''Is coffee ready? I could use a cup.''

She nodded without replying. When he returned with two steaming mugs and the milk and sugar he spoke again with renewed vigor.

''Nadine, I had a hell of a time when I got married. I had an even worse time getting divorced. You've no idea what the divorce courts are like in Italy, especially when the divorce is being contested. But in spite of the awful time I had I'm willing to commit myself to you. I'm not going to let my cynicism and bitterness interfere with the way I feel about you. You should be equally willing to put your cynicism and resentment behind you and start again.''

Nadine sipped the hot coffee. ''That doesn't necessarily follow,'' she objected slowly. ''Your disastrous relationship was with another woman. If I'd been betrayed by another man, then you came along and offered to marry me, I wouldn't necessarily blame you for the other guy's betrayal. But my problem is that I'd be stepping right back into our old relationship, and that's the one that I can't seem to get over, even now.''

''Remember, I was just as devastated by your leaving me as you were by my 'betrayal,' as you call it. But I'm willing to forgive you.''

''Not 'just as,' '' she replied.

"I think so. Although I didn't have a pregnancy and financial difficulties to contend with, so maybe I recovered more quickly. But I bet if you hadn't had to struggle with Jamie and poverty, you would have gotten over me too."

"No," she asserted, positively.

"You don't credit me with much feeling," he said wryly.

Her eyes smiled, but her voice was sad.

"It's not that."

"What is it, then? Why won't you consider marrying me?"

"Maybe it's because I credit you with too much feeling for too many women."

"Nadine." He sighed. "I admit I was a fool, but so were you, if you'll remember. I'm willing to forget and forgive. Why can't you?"

"I have more to lose." The flames were low in the grate now, and the jumpy shadows licked the high ceiling and opposite wall erratically.

"You'll have Jamie; I won't."

She accepted his assertion without doubt. "I'm no longer afraid of that. But there are other things. I don't want to become dependent on anyone else, because I'm not sure that I could stand being torn from what I'm dependent on again." She took another sip of coffee, reflectively. "Maybe four years ago living with you was an adventure that I risked without much thought because I fell in love with you. It was romantic and exciting. But not now. Now the thought only terrifies me. I have to protect Jamie as well as myself. I have to be cautious."

"I'm that unreliable?"

She gave an uncertain shrug. "Your feelings toward relationships are different from mine. You fall in and out of love without a blink; you can make love with dozens of women and say you love them all; you can marry one of those women because you think you're honor-bound to do so, and when you learn you're not honor-bound you declare yourself free of the relationship. I'll bet you told Lily you loved her, though. Don't you think you've hurt her? Don't you imagine how much she must have loved you, to trick you into marrying her? You're capable of a great deal of hurt because of your unwillingness to take responsibility for your relationships. Lily, me, yourself—we've all been hurt. I won't let you hurt Jamie.''

Lawrence set down his coffee cup sharply, his mouth set in a grim line. He rose and paced up and down the small room impatiently, and Nadine nervously wondered if she had broken the rational intimacy of their conversation. But he turned to her finally and broke out:

''You've absurdly exaggerated my behavior! Why do you keep making me defend myself? I'm sorry. I've said I'm sorry. I was ignorant, selfish, stupid—I've agreed to all that. But I've changed. I know I hurt you; I won't do it again. And you've changed too. You were a spoiled, immature, unreasonable kid when you were in Florence, and that side of you came out more and more when you realized that I meant what I said about not wanting any kind of commitment from you. You simply can't go on believing that I was solely to blame for our breakup.'' He stopped pacing and stood before her. ''Now try and be practical. You'd be gaining security, not losing it. You'd be gaining a family life, and Jamie would too. You could put your energy into your thesis. You could be financially secure, living in the city that I know you love, with your son, and with the man who loves you.'' He sat down beside her again. ''He's always loved you, Nadine. He's never stopped loving you. There's never been another woman who meant what you mean to me. I want to take responsibility for you and Jamie, and I won't let you down.''

Nadine was trembling from Lawrence's impassioned words. How she had longed hear him declare his love all these years! Florence—the villa—her master's degree—Jamie running freely through the poppies and dandelions and tall grass in the paradisal field—and Lawrence, all the time, day in and day out. The offer was a glorious one! But she had loved him so terribly years ago—and it hadn't worked then.

Rain pattered on the glass window panes. She felt as though she were floating on stormy clouds of elation and grief.

"I'm glad," she said at last. "I'm glad you love me. Now you know how it feels. You never understood how much I suffered when you went off with Lily. Now you do."

"Okay," he replied quietly. "So you've had your revenge. You loved me then; I love you now. If we lived together, committed to one another, maybe you could learn to love me again. We might still be happy together. You told me in Florence that security was more important to you than love. Now you tell me you used to love me but you don't anymore. I'm not asking you to love me. I'm asking you to accept the security I'm offering you for your sake and for Jamie's sake. We'll both be getting what we want most in life. You want security and I want you."

The blood sang in her ears. She put out her hand, palm up. His long, square-tipped fingers closed over it reverently.

"Lawrence," she began huskily, a lump forming in her throat. Electrical currents darted up her arm from his touch. She turned toward him slowly, legs tucked under her, and her free hand crept around the back of his head. She leaned toward him and buried her lips in the strong column of his neck, feeling the rapid hammering of his pulse. She unbuttoned his shirt and ran her fingers through the thick, soft hair on his chest. He groaned.

"Sweetheart—" His mouth found her ear, and several successive tremors ran through her. She wanted him—more than anything. She pressed her body against his, trembling.

"Might Jamie wake up?" he whispered between kisses.

"No," she murmured. "He was tired."

He gently pulled off her sweater, and the dim firelight played on her pale breasts.

"Beautiful—beautiful Nadine," he muttered.

They moved to the bed in the far corner of the room, leaving their clothes where they were. Fire played in Nadine's bones, sending rapturous shivers through her. The bed creaked beneath their weight. Lawrence's heavy-lidded eyes gazed passionately at her.

"Say it," he ordered huskily.

She didn't understand immediately, and puzzlement shadowed her eyes.

His mouth crushed against hers, then moved down her throat to her chest. "I love you," he exclaimed, fiercely and softly. "I love you, Nadine Barnet."

That he longed to hear the same words from her lips was evident by the slight pause following his declaration. When she didn't speak he continued his exquisite assault on her body.

"Lawrence, please—" she cried. She could yield her body, her passionate desire for him, but she could not tell him yet that she loved him.

At last he found the throbbing center of her rapture. Within seconds she exploded in a fierce, shattering wave of ecstasy. He rocked her back and forth, and cried out her name in a muffled voice. He held her tightly as though he could not bear to let her go.

Nadine clung to him also. Their bodies were damp; Lawrence brushed a strand of hair from her sweaty brow, still breathing heavily.

When they had both grown still and lay in each other's arms, Lawrence lifted himself onto one elbow and gazed down at Nadine's flushed face in the light from the streetlamp outside. One hand coursed its way down the smooth cheek to her mouth, and she kissed it. He said slowly:

"Before I met you I never knew what it was like to open your heart to someone. I tried when I was a child, first to my father, who left us, then to my mother, who treated me abominably most of the time. I soon learned how not to feel simply in order to protect myself. The only time I felt close to letting myself experience freely, without reservation, was when I painted, but even there I felt a coldness that I don't like to remember now. Then I met you, Nadine. You were so open, so self-confident, so willing to love, and so certain of being loved in return. You trusted me to love you and cherish you in a way that I had never trusted anyone. I think that's why I kept saying I didn't want any commitment. That wasn't strictly true, I don't think. It was more that I was frightened you'd give yourself utterly to me, and keep nothing for yourself. I could see the danger, because that's what I'd done myself when I was a kid. But in spite of that, you kept on giving more and more and more. That's what I remembered all these years, sweetheart. Not your tantrums, or the fights we used to have, but your total giving of yourself. You were stronger than I because you weren't afraid of giving yourself. But I gave enough of myself to be devastated by your departure, and I was determined to try and heal the breach. That's why I wrote that first letter. It took a hell of a lot for me to do it, although I know you never realized the effort it cost me. Your letter was just the confirmation I needed that if I opened my heart to someone it would be rejected.''

"I'm sorry," Nadine interjected softly. "I'm so sorry."

"Still, I remembered how open and affectionate and un-afraid you were, and so I wrote again. No response was worse than getting an angry response, because I assumed it meant indifference. I may have married Lily out of sense of duty, but it was also because you rejected my peace offering.'' Imagining his hurt, believing it for the first time, Nadine's mouth trembled as she felt the tears well up. Seeing this, he kissed her, smiling gently. "Don't look so depressed. Even if you didn't love me anymore, I was determined to learn your lesson. I could feel again: I had learned how to feel, and how to express that feeling. You noticed something different in my paintings when you returned last month, remember? I think that's what it was: It was as though the floodgates to my innermost feelings had been opened and not only could I feel, I could paint! It was a wonderful thing.''

Nadine willed her tears away, closing her eyes.

"It worked out differently for me, I guess," she said after a silence. "I used to be the way you described. Now I'm uncertain, insecure, and one thing I've learned is control over my emotions. I don't give my affection and loyalty as I used to."

She heard his voice but didn't open her eyes.

"Self-control isn't such a bad thing. And just because you can control your emotions, it doesn't mean you don't have them or they aren't as deep as they were. With me it was different. I'd forgotten how to feel. I didn't have anything to control."

She gave a nod, feeling a poignant mixture of dizzying sadness and elation in her breast. Lawrence took her in his arms again so that her hot cheek rested on the soft dark hair of his broad chest.

"Come to Florence," he whispered. "We'll make it work. It will be glorious."

There was a long silence. She listened to his heart pounding against her ear as though she were listening to the ocean in a large sea shell.

"All right," she replied at last. "I'll marry you."

Lawrence caught his breath in a perceptible relief from tension. He sealed her promise with a tender kiss and enfolded her in his strong arms.

"We'll get married before we leave."

Nadine closed her eyes, hardly daring to think of what had just happened. She was actually going to marry Lawrence Stebbing. Jamie's father. This was what she had secretly longed for ever since their parting. But even so she felt uneasy. Was she making the right decision? Could she afford to risk her—and Jamie's—security for the man who had let her down once already?

"Don't tell Jamie yet," she asked suddenly.

"Why not?"

"I think we should wait a few days."

Her heart was beating as rapidly and unsteadily as that of a frightened deer. Lawrence kissed her again. Nadine tried to quell her unreasonable panic at the commitment she had just made.

Neither of them slept well. A pale gray dawn lightened the small room at last, and, overwrought from the emotional conversation of the night before, they rose and had an early-morning cup of coffee. In the dim light of morning all the apartment's drabness returned, and Nadine thought with a frayed heart of the promised heaven of Fiesole.

They did not speak about last night's conversation again. Jamie awoke soon after they did, and Lawrence kept up an interested bantering conversation with his son. They might have been a regular, happy little family, Nadine thought, pouring Lawrence more coffee.

Lawrence offered to take Jamie to school, and Nadine gave him the spare key to her apartment. There was no reason why he shouldn't pick up Jamie as well later that afternoon.

"See you tonight then?" Lawrence asked softly, kissing her cheek in farewell.

She nodded, hugged Jamie goodbye, and watched father and son go down the stairs hand in hand. Her heart contracted in love and in a lingering uncertainty and fear.

Charlotte and Steve had invited them for dinner again the following evening. Nadine had finally agreed to announce their engagement at dinner.

Lawrence and Jamie were already at Nadine's apartment when she got home at five-thirty, and they greeted her warmly. After a quick cup of tea and a rundown on the day's events, Nadine went into Jamie's room to dress. Lawrence followed her. His arms wrapped around her as she slipped into her flat black shoes.

"What happened to your fantastic wardrobe?" he asked

teasingly, glancing into the open closet. "I was beginning to think you had one room only for clothes."

She replied absently, "Oh, those were all my sister's. She used to be skinnier."

Lawrence chewed his lip thoughtfully but made no rejoinder. He was wearing sherry-colored wide cord pants and his green shetland sweater over a white shirt. Nadine's eyes traveled over his slim thighs to his broad chest and felt a sudden rush of love and desire. She put down her brush and rested her cheek against his chest. He folded his arms around her comfortingly.

"Nadine, let's tell your parents that you're getting married. Wouldn't you like them to be at the ceremony? It'd be the perfect opportunity for a reconciliation."

She extricated herself from his hold and returned to the mirror to finish brushing her hair.

"Forget it," she said, eyeing his reflection in the mirror.

"Why?"

"They let me down in a worse way than you did. I can't forgive them."

"How did they let you down? You never told me." He regarded her reflection on the mirror gravely.

"They didn't forgive me for being unmarried and pregnant. They didn't even want to *know* about Jamie. If it hadn't been for Charlotte—" She brushed her hair so hard that it hurt.

He came up behind her again and wrapped his arms around her waist. "Oh, baby," he muttered, kissing her shiny hair. "How awful."

"It was awful."

He rallied. "But now you will be married. They're probably dying for an excuse to see you again."

"If they need an excuse, then let them find one," she replied sharply, extricating herself from his arms.

"Don't you think you're being unreasonable?"

Her eyes flashed. "No! I don't want to go running back to

them now and tell them that I've finally taken their advice and gotten married! I'm not marrying you for their sakes!''

"I didn't say you were," he protested mildly. "I'm just suggesting a reconciliation. I'm not saying you have to take any blame or accept forgiveness for what happened. I bet they don't either; they'd probably just as soon forget it."

"*I'd* just as soon forget it," she snapped.

"But you aren't giving them a chance. Just as you refused to give me a chance until I forced it on you."

"When *they* force it on me, I'll reconsider," she said coldly.

"But you can't still be angry at them!" he said disbelievingly.

"I'm not angry; I just don't think about them. And I have no intention of doing so." She broke off when she saw Jamie standing in the doorway. He was already dressed for dinner, wearing blue corduroy pants, a red sweater, and sneakers that Lawrence had bought him. The change in Jamie since Lawrence had appeared on the scene was remarkable, Nadine had to admit. Her eyes softened.

"Don't be angry, Mommy," Jamie said seriously, going over to her. "Lawrence didn't mean anything bad." He looked anxiously at Lawrence for assurance.

For Jamie's sake Nadine bit back her angry retort to Lawrence's words and smiled at him.

"Okay, sweetheart. Are you ready to go to Aunt Char's?"

"Yup."

Glancing at Lawrence, she saw a tender, amused look in his eyes that melted her heart in spite of her irritation.

"Let's go then," she suggested. They could discuss the issue of a reconciliation later, when Jamie wasn't around.

But unfortunately over the lavish dinner that Charlotte had prepared the same topic was unwittingly introduced by her overjoyed sister.

"Mom and Dad will be so pleased that you're getting

married! It'll be a perfect way of getting you guys back together again! Don't you think so, Lawrence?''

Before he had a chance to reply, Nadine shot back angrily:

''Forget it, Charlotte. You know they wouldn't care one way or the other. And if they do care, so much the better! Let them be hurt. As far as I'm concerned, they're dead.''

Charlotte looked shocked. ''Don't say that,'' she ordered hastily, glancing around to make sure all the children were out of earshot.

Lawrence intervened. ''I happened to have broached this same subject just before we came here,'' he said lightly, throwing a warning glance at Nadine. ''Nadine probably thinks we're ganging up on her, trying to make her do something she isn't ready for. Let's change the subject.''

Steve helped him out.

''When are you planning to move to Florence?'' he asked innocently. He didn't understand the hostile look Nadine threw him. ''What's the matter?''

''Why do you assume we're moving to Florence?'' she asked, ashamed of her uncontrolled outbursts, but unable to suppress her indignation. ''I suppose it's because I'm a woman and I'm duty-bound to follow my husband wherever he dictates? As a matter of fact we haven't decided where we're going to live, but there's no reason why it should be Florence instead of New York.''

Charlotte stared at Nadine's sharp tone; Lawrence gripped his wineglass and eyed his hands; Steve stood up.

''Come help me make the coffee,'' he suggested kindly to Nadine. ''Char, dear, want to move into the living room?''

Obediently, she stood up, and Lawrence followed suit. Nadine sullenly followed Steve into the kitchen. While he got out the cups and saucers for coffee, he said:

''You don't seem entirely happy with the decision you've made to marry Lawrence. You know your sister and I wouldn't advise you to do anything that goes against your inclination. Maybe you should reconsider.''

"Are you saying you don't trust my judgment in that matter either?" she retorted sarcastically.

"No, I'm not saying that," he replied patiently.

"Why can't you all leave me alone?" she burst out. "I don't need your advice, I don't need my parents, I don't need to be told I should go to Florence! I've done enough figuring out of my own life over the past few years to be able to take care of myself!"

"No one's saying you can't take care of yourself. We're just trying to help."

"Don't try to help, then!" she cried furiously. "Why should I go crawling back to my parents to tell them that I'm finally going to do what they wanted me to do all along— marry Jamie's father? I'm not marrying him for their sakes! And I'm not marrying him to make up for any stupid sin they think I committed by living with him without being married!"

Lawrence appeared in the doorway. She was about to lash out at him also, but a suppressed fury in his dark green eyes made her reconsider.

"Let's go," he said, his voice even. "I don't want to spend an evening tiptoing around avoiding a fight, and I certainly don't want to be responsible for subjecting Steve and Charlotte to your bad temper." He glanced at Steve, who was uncomfortably arranging cups on a silver tray. "We'll come back for coffee some other time."

Steve nodded unhappily. "Sure."

"Get Jamie," Lawrence ordered Nadine. She did not rebel against his curt demand, but turned on her heel and headed for the den, angry at his highhanded behavior, but a little scared as well. She was only too aware of Lawrence's suppressed wrath.

She was silent in the cab ride back to her apartment, and half-listened to Lawrence talking with Jamie.

"Do you always watch television with your cousins?" he asked.

Jamie sat between them, as though separating them from

explosive physical contact. Nadine was grateful for the barrier, small as it was, and stared out the dark window into Central Park, thinking her own thoughts. She was ashamed of her outburst. Surely she was not the kind of woman Lawrence would want to marry, not now that he saw what she was really like.

Jamie replied, "I draw sometimes."

"But don't you play games together?"

Nadine heard resignation in Jamie's voice. "Sometimes. But games always end up in fights. TV is safer."

So Jamie too wanted things safe, Nadine thought unhappily. Had she instilled in him her own longing for security, although he was so young?

Once they were in her apartment, she tucked Jamie into bed and kissed him goodnight. Sensitive to her feelings as he always was, Jamie asked:

"Mommy, are you angry?"

She met his questioning, green eyes openly. "No, dear, I'm not angry with you."

He nodded wisely. "You must be angry at Lawrence then. He looked sad tonight." He snuggled down under the blankets and turned over onto his side. "I'm sorry for Lawrence," he added, "because it's terrible when you're angry at someone. I'm glad it's not me."

Nadine hesitated, kissed the side of his face again, and said gently:

"I'm not angry at Lawrence." Jamie's sympathy was obviously entirely with his father.

"Is he angry at you?"

"A little, yes."

A smile lit his sleepy face. "That's okay, because nobody can be really angry at you because you're too nice."

Little did he know, Nadine thought to herself, straightening. To her embarrassment, Lawrence stood in the doorway, listening. She slipped past him without speaking, and he went over to Jamie's bedside.

"Goodnight, son," he said quietly.

Jamie eyed him warily. "You're not really angry with Mommy, are you?"

He shook his head. "No, son, I'm not." He leaned over to kiss him. "Goodnight," he whispered. He closed the door softly behind him.

Nadine sat on the couch in front of the cold fireplace and regarded him with an odd mixture of contrition and defiance. Lawrence took off his sweater, poured himself a glass of scotch, and got some ice from the freezer, then settled himself in the armchair, at some distance from her. Lines of tiredness had settled under his eyes and on his brow, and his mouth was drawn. Expecting him to blast her as he had in her sister's kitchen, Nadine was unprepared for his first words:

"I'm going to ask you a question. Answer from your heart. No games, no lies, all right?" She nodded. "What do you think I'm thinking right now?"

Her lips parted in surprise. From her heart, he had said. What did she truly think was uppermost in his mind? She bowed her head, humiliated.

"You think I'm an unreasonable, hysterical, immature idiot, and you want to change your mind about marrying me." Her voice was barely audible.

He gave a deep sigh, full of weariness. She waited for his agreement. Instead, he moved to sit next to her on the couch. She felt the springs sink under his weight, but still she could not look up. His voice was heavy:

"I thought you'd say that. Everything you said tonight has been designed to push me to my limits, as though you're trying to prove to me that there's no way I could like you enough to marry you. I was to call off the engagement so you could act like a martyr all over again, saying to yourself I'm still the selfish, untrustworthy deserter I was four years ago. You're begging to be put in the position of being a martyr, Nadine. Why?"

He could hardly hear her response. "I'm not. I didn't mean it like that."

He took another sip of scotch. "I'm sure you weren't conscious of your motive. Still, that's what you were doing. Why? Why don't you think that you deserve me, or I you?"

The black, empty grate in the hearth dissolved before her eyes, and she blinked madly to keep it in focus. She concentrated on it almost with desperation, outlining the flakes of soot clinging to the metal grid, etching the black bricks in the wall behind in her mind. Lawrence reached out and took both her hands in his. She felt overpowered by the large, long fingers, the muscular palms. She turned her eyes to his hands, and they too were washed from her sight. Angrily she tried to bring them back into focus. Her own hands had disappeared in his, and she felt as small and helpless as they were.

Her voice was slightly breathless. "I don't think I'll ever be able to feel any other way, I'll always be the way I am now: insecure, uncertain of your fidelity, not sure if you really do love me, or whether you're marrying me because of Jamie, or because you feel sorry for me—" She gulped. "It's not just because of what happened between us before, it's because my parents let me down too. I never imagined them turning on me like that. You have no idea of the panic I felt! I was so afraid I wouldn't be able to make it on my own."

"But you have made it on your own." He gripped her hands more tightly. She felt crushed.

"Yes. But the price I paid was too high for me to risk going through something like that again. I don't want to depend on you or my parents or anyone, ever again. And falling in love is a kind of dependence." She swallowed again past an aching throat. "That's why I don't want to see my parents again: I know I'll forgive them and start needing them again, and counting on them in my old silly way."

"Forget your parents." His voice was hoarse. "What about me?"

"But you're the same thing. If I married you I wouldn't just be having sex and a grand old time, I'd start to need you, to count on you, to depend on you for everything that I've had to depend on myself for since I left you. But all the time I'd be terrified that I might be thrown out into the world on my own again, and this time I'd have Jamie to protect too. Marriage won't rid me of my insecurity about you." She swallowed again and bowed her head lower. "I can't marry you, Lawrence. It wouldn't change my feelings. I thought I could do it, but I can't." And the hands that gripped hers so powerfully dissolved into a dim, hazy glow again.

His answer was the closing seal to the end of their relationship. "I know," was all he said.

She forced the tears from her eyes again, determined not to break down. She was past tears, wasn't she? Not even tears could fill this hollow ache of loneliness in hearing his quiet agreement that she could not marry him. Finally she gazed up at him, wanting to show him that she was not crying, to prove to him that she was strong and independent and brave, that she could bear this final parting stoically. But he didn't see her look at him. His own eyes were blind with unshed tears.

"I won't forgive myself for destroying your faith and your trust in those you love," he said hoarsely. "But you expected too much, Nadine. I'm just a man. I can't even promise that if we did marry I'd never hurt you again. I've got weaknesses, failings, parts of myself that I despise, and if you can't live with them, it won't work." He rose abruptly, dropping her hands as though they burned him, and turned his back to her, his broad shoulders hunched. Her heart contracted. She stood up too and put a hand on his shoulder.

"Lawrence," she began.

He supported himself with both hands, leaning heavily on the kitchen table, as though too weak to stand straight. Brokenly he pleaded:

"Don't."

She retreated to the sofa, bewildered by his grief. For some time they remained like that, in silence.

Lawrence stirred first. He picked up his glass of scotch, took too large a gulp, and coughed. Nadine sped to his side and slapped him hard on his back. When he caught his breath, they both began laughing grimly, facing each other. He gripped her wrists and then his mouth found hers and they kissed each other desperately.

Their deep frustration turned into a struggle for physical possession. This was the Nadine she used to be: uninhibited, challenging, tender, and terribly exciting. Her breasts pressed against his broad chest, her tongue flicked eagerly over his ear, his throat, his teeth and tongue.

Unrestrainedly she undressed him where he stood on the hard kitchen floor. Tantalized beyond endurance by her teasing, wild mouth, Lawrence picked her up roughly and carried her to the bed, then tugged off her trousers savagely.

With relentless determination, he proceeded to cover her entire body with kisses. Nadine begged for release, and finally took over, exciting him with equal abandon. He pulled her onto his hips and she straddled him, surveying the glorious animal-like hair that covered his body from behind lowered lids.

"Love me," he ordered hoarsely. "Oh, God, love me!"

She complied. Their bodies wrestled to become one. They rocked to a blissful, demanding rhythm of lovemaking, rolling around on the bed in a frenzy of passion.

Nadine felt as though Lawrence were staking a claim on her body. He demanded physical possession of her body if he couldn't have her heart and soul. A storm of electrical currents fought for release inside her. Taking her with him to a feverish crescendo, Lawrence plundered her as though somewhere deep inside he might discover and steal her safely locked-up heart.

She was still shaking with the remains of her passion when at last he collapsed on top of her.

"What is it, sweetheart?" His arms wrapped protectively around her. He was still breathless, but his voice was worried. "I didn't hurt you, did I?"

"No." Her reply was muffled in his chest. "It was just— too much—"

He held her tightly in his arms.

"There must be a way of starting over," he muttered, gritting his teeth in frustration. "I won't give up. I won't."

Chapter Eleven

The next morning Nadine awoke and found herself alone. Tired but exhilarated from their savage lovemaking of the night before, she stretched and looked around the shabby room. Where was Lawrence? No sound emanated from the bathroom, or from Jamie's room. She rose and slipped on her bathrobe. On the kitchen table she found a hastily scrawled note from Lawrence:

"We're off to school—I'll be back in half an hour. We didn't want to wake you."

Unconsciously she parted her lips in a half-smile, imagining them tiptoeing around the kitchen fixing breakfast, whispering conspiratorially so that she would be allowed to sleep. She turned to make some coffee, feeling relaxed and lighthearted. A cold rain fell heavily onto the drab street outside, a sharp contrast from yesterday's Indian summer. She hugged the bathrobe around her waist, wondering at her strange feeling of relief and happiness. Had the fact that they both agreed she could not marry Lawrence lifted her spirits like this? It didn't make any sense.

The coffee was ready. She poured herself a cup and sat at the small table, watching the rain spattering the small window. How could she stand another winter here? How could she bear the cold, the loneliness, her tedious job, and her anxiety for Jamie's safety? She would not be sacrificing much to give that up, would she? The early-morning gloom filled her with longing for Lawrence's return. Wasn't she strong enough to maintain her independence and to love him also? She almost thought she was.

The key turned in the lock. Dripping wet, Lawrence stood on the threshold. Her heart jumped at the sight of him, his dark hair plastered to his head, the shoulders of his jacket and his knees soaked with rain.

"Good morning." She smiled. "Coffee?"

Lawrence looked as though he had not slept at all. His unshaven jaw and the shadows below his eyes made him look gaunt and exhausted. "I'd love a cup." He took off his wet jacket, shook it, then ran his hand unconsciously through his wet hair. He sat down.

Nadine set the cup in front of him. Couldn't she tell him she would go with him to Florence? Hesitantly she kissed the top of his rain-soaked head, rubbing the back of his neck affectionately as she did so. But she couldn't bring herself to speak.

He caught her hand and gripped it tightly.

"I've been thinking all night what to do," he said quickly. "There's only one solution I can come up with. I've gone around and around—" Nadine waited while he took a sip of coffee. She should have trusted Lawrence to think of a solution, she thought gratefully. "I'm going back to Florence. Alone. Today. I'm leaving you to decide for yourself whether or not you'll join me there with Jamie."

Nadine's face drained of color, and she withdrew her hand stiffly. Unable to speak, she turned to the little window. Desertion again. She should have expected it.

She could feel Lawrence's eyes fixed on her rigid back.

"You know I want you to come with me, but I'm not going to try and persuade you again. If you do decide to come, it has to be of your own free will, and on your own responsibility. I don't want you to blame me if anything goes wrong, or if you're unhappy there. The only way you can live with me is if you yourself take full responsibility for making the decision.''

She did not turn around, did not speak. She didn't fully comprehend what he said; all she knew was that Lawrence was leaving her—again.

His hands rested on her shoulders and forced her to turn around to face him.

"Nadine," he said quietly, "I've been going about trying to win your love in entirely the wrong way. I thought I could persuade you to love me, persuade you to trust me. That's all wrong. Any trust you feel or love you might eventually feel has to come from inside you. Do you understand?" When she still made no sign, he added, "You know that what I want most of all in the world is to be with you and Jamie. But I won't stay in New York trying to prove to you that it's true, because even if eventually I succeed you still won't have taken your share of the responsibility for our relationship.''

With an effort she kept her voice even. "You're probably making the right decision for us both by going back. Better sooner than later.''

He dropped his hands from her shoulders. "You're misunderstanding me. By going back I'm deliberately not making a decision for you. I'm leaving the decision entirely up to you.''

"It's not a fair choice." Inwardly she wept; outwardly she was controlled. "You're asking me to risk too much.''

"I love you. Don't you know what that means? I give you my life. Can't you trust me with yours?''

She grasped almost wildly for self-control.

"The decision you're asking me to make has nothing to do with love or with trust. It has to do with human nature. Our natures. I need security; you need independence. The fact that you love me doesn't necessarily mean you can live with me. And the fact that I love you—" She stopped abruptly. She loved him so much she thought her heart would break. "Don't you see, Lawrence: That's the tragedy we're faced with. Not unrequited love or lack of trust or suspicion, but the fact that we can't live together. Love has nothing to do with our incompatibility.''

"Love has everything to do with it," he said earnestly.

"Last time love got the better of us, look what happened."

"That was a different kind of love. I fell in love with your naiveté, your enthusiasm, your admiration for me. And you were infatuated with an experienced, famous artist, a rescuer from the wet streets of Florence. We don't feel that way any longer. I love *you:* a courageous, mature, strong-hearted, loyal woman who has suffered because of me." He took a breath. "The same goes for you. If you love me now, it's a man you love, not an illusion."

"I was never in love with an illusion."

"If you weren't, then you wouldn't have been so badly hurt by me. If you hadn't gilded me with a heroic, impossibly virtuous nature, you wouldn't have been surprised to discover that in actual fact I was just a man."

Nadine collapsed on the rickety wooden chair and clenched her fists despairingly. She broke out passionately:

"You're the one that doesn't understand! Can't you see it makes no difference whether I loved an illusion or not? I loved you so terribly! I can't go through it again!"

After a brief silence Lawrence said in a softened voice:

"Could you love the man I really am as terribly as you once loved the man you thought I was? It's much easier to love a hero, and easier to be let down by one too."

She lifted her stormy, glistening eyes to his forest-dark ones.

"I always loved the same man," she insisted. "The nature of my love may have changed, but the object of it never will."

And that was the end of their conversation. Nadine walked Lawrence downstairs to the covered front porch of her building. They stood under the gray shelter. Sooty rain fell heavily on the dismal street and dirty parked cars.

An empty cab came slowly down the street. In the sudden realization of their eminent separation, they found themselves locked in an unexpected embrace, so tight neither could breathe.

As quickly, both let go.

"Goodbye—" He walked down the five stone steps and hailed the cab.

"Goodbye," she whispered.

The bright yellow cab drove off and disappeared in the gray wet world beyond. Nadine turned and walked slowly back upstairs to her apartment. She closed and locked the door behind her, gazing around at the grimly empty apartment.

How could she bear this final separation? She loved him; she had never stopped loving him. Seeing him again had brought to the surface the passion she had fought to suppress since the night she had left him in Florence. How could he have betrayed her again with this decision to leave?

A sob caught in her throat. How could she live without him? He was dearer than life. She pressed her hand to her mouth, unable to stifle the anguished cry from her heart.

"Lawrence—"

She collapsed on a hard chair and buried her face in her arms, overwhelmed by a storm of bitter weeping.

It was several nights after Lawrence's departure. Jamie was tucked into bed and had been asleep for hours. The weather had turned sharply cold the last few days, and Nadine folded her arms against her soft wool sweater, shivering.

She stared irresolutely at the telephone. Lawrence had not called, and she longed to hear his voice. She also longed for his reassurance that he still wanted her if she decided to come to Florence, but she was nervous about calling him. Would he be angry if she did not have a definite answer?

Still, he couldn't expect her to be able to make the choice entirely by herself, could he? She had to talk to him. She picked up the telephone and asked the international operator for Lawrence's number.

To her shocked amazement a woman answered. Suddenly Nadine realized that it must be very early in the morning in Florence. What was a woman doing in Lawrence's house? Had he let her down already?

"*Dica pura*?" the voice asked. Nadine shook herself. Perhaps she had gotten the wrong number.

She cleared her throat. "Is Lawrence there?" She hoped the woman understood English.

"No, I am sorry. Who is calling?"

Even after all these years Nadine could not mistake the sexy cadences of that rich, lovely voice. Lily! Lily was sleeping in Lawrence's villa!

She willed herself to speak. "This is Nadine Barnet."

"Nadine!" Lily was evidently amazed to hear her voice. "You are in Florence?"

"No. I'm calling from New York."

"New York? That is too far away, Nadine!" Lily's voice was perfectly cordial. "You should come back to Florence."

"I was thinking about it," she returned noncommittally.

"I remember how much you loved Florence," Lily continued. "You stayed away a long time. We will look forward very much to seeing you."

We look forward, Nadine thought, a stab of fear plunging into her breast. Had Lily and Lawrence reconciled? She cleared her throat again.

"Nothing's definite. I wanted to talk to Lawrence."

"I will tell him you called," Lily assured her, sounding regretful.

"Thanks. Sorry to disturb you."

"No problem." She could almost see Lily smile. "I hope we see you soon. Florence is lovely at this time of year."

Replacing the receiver, Nadine felt a bitter ache settle in her bones. How could she have fooled herself that Lawrence meant what he said about not letting her down again? He would never change; he would never be faithful to her. Why had she imagined he was any different?

Agitated and thoroughly depressed, she prowled the small apartment. Anger at Lawrence welled up inside her, and the hours crept by with lonely slowness.

She went to bed at last but was unable to sleep. Her half-formed dream of returning to Florence was shattered. She stared, dry-eyed, at the shadowed ceiling. Damn Lawrence, she thought. He had spoiled everything.

Suddenly Nadine sat up in bed. Had Lawrence really spoiled the possibility of her moving to Italy? He had made their living together impossible, but what prevented her from living in Florence with Jamie? He did not own Florence.

Excitedly she rose, tied the sash of her dressing gown around her waist, and switched on the lamp on the kitchen table. Lily's words came back to her. "I remember how much you loved Florence," she had said, and by doing so had reminded Nadine herself how much she had loved the exquisite Tuscan city. The hell with Lawrence—she and Jamie would move there on their own!

She boiled water for coffee, her mind racing at this new possibility. It might really work! She had enough in her savings account to pay for their flight to Italy and for a few days' stay in a *pensione*. Lawrence could not be trusted to be faithful to her, but she knew without question that she could trust him to provide for Jamie. She herself could find work at the university while she studied for her master's degree. It could work!

Her anger abated. She sipped her coffee, her eyes cloudy with doubt and excitement. Had the thought that she would be living with Lawrence, sleeping in his arms, watching him paint, walking, talking, making love—had that been her prime motivation for wanting to live in Florence? Would she be happy living in the same city as Lawrence, but apart from him, loving him as she did?

It was strange, she thought, cradling the hot mug of coffee

in her hands, but even the knowledge of Lawrence's infidelity no longer made her feel bitter. A new fountain of light-filled love had sprung up from deep inside her, and she knew she would love him no matter what he did. For the rest of her life she would love him, with a passion that no longer frightened her but filled her with a quiet joy. She loved Lawrence with an emotion far deeper than she had felt when she was twenty, and she knew that in the years to come it would grow stronger yet.

The next night Nadine and Jamie sat companionably at the kitchen table after dinner. She watched Jamie's light brown hair bent over a large notepad she had splurged on that afternoon, the tip of his pink tongue poking out one side of his mouth, his brow concentratedly frowning. He asked suddenly without looking up:

"When will we see Lawrence again?"

She set her elbows on the table, regarding him curiously.

"Do you want to, darling?"

"Oh, yes."

"Would you like to leave New York?" she asked, taking a breath.

He looked up. "Where would we go?"

"To Italy. That's where your father and I first met, and that's where he still lives." She took another breath. "Let me tell you a little about it. He lives in a little city in the heart of Tuscany. The hills around are a coppery gold and sparkling green, just like your eyes. The sky is the prettiest blue you can imagine. It's where some of the greatest drawings and paintings and statues in the world are kept. There's a little river that runs through the city. One of the bridges has shops and little houses on it. . . ." Her eyes half-closed and her voice grew dreamy. "Then there's the house where Lawrence lives. It's outside of the city, in the countryside. The garden is small, but there's a large field of wild flowers in the back to play in. There's a forest at the edge of that field, and a stream running through it. The house is the most beautiful building you've ever seen. It's tall and old and the stones are a deep orange-pink when the sun hits them in the evening Inside there's a big living room, about four times the size of our whole apartment here. Then there's another big room to sleep in on the second floor. Lawrence draws and paints on the top floor, where he's got the best light. There's a nightingale that sings all night long in the woods at the edge of the field; you can hear it when you sit on the terrace overlooking the field. The sun rises directly over it so that when there's been dew the whole world sparkles like precious jewels.''

Jamie's voice reached her, as though from far away. She focused her gaze on him and saw him staring at her, rapt, as though he actually saw what she had described.

"It sounds nice." The awe in his voice lent emphasis to the simple adjective.

The next day Nadine handed in her resignation to Everett, adding that she hoped he would not mind if she did not give him the usual two weeks' notice. She did not satisfy his curiosity regarding her plans, but merely said that she wasn't happy with the school Jamie was attending, and felt it was imperative she spend more time with him. Try as he might, he could extract no more information than that, although when she told him that Lawrence had returned to Italy he looked surprised. After a cursory attempt to dissuade her he let her go.

After work that day Nadine headed up to her sister's to pick up Jamie for the last time.

"What's happened to you?" Charlotte cried when she saw her. "You look as though you've just won this week's lottery!"

Nadine fairly danced into the room. It was as though a great weight had been lifted from her shoulders now she had made the decision never to return to the Mills Gallery.

"I've quit!" she announced, beaming at her sister.

Charlotte was not as overjoyed as she was.

"Did you get another job?"

"Nope."

"You're too impulsive, Nadine. What are you going to do now?"

Nadine dropped her tweed jacket on the back of a chair, made a pirouette on the plush blue rug, and gave a mocking curtsy to her sister, who stood with pursed lips by the kitchen door.

"I'm going to Florence, Char! Jamie and I are moving there."

"With Lawrence?" Charlotte gasped. "You are getting married, then!"

"Nope; Jamie and I are going to live by ourselves." She flung her jacket on to a chair.

"But why? Did he change his mind about marrying you?"

Nadine shrugged. "I don't know. I haven't talked to him. But Jamie and I are moving to Florence and we're going to live by ourselves."

Not even Charlotte's anxiousness could depress her. She caught her sister's plump, smooth hands in hers and regarded her with a glow in her eyes.

"You know what, Char? I feel as though I've been freed from something that was hanging around my neck these past four years. Like an albatross. Now I feel as I used to in college and before that. I can do anything, go anywhere, with no one to answer to, no one to reprimand me, nothing to lose! I was wrong to think I had to change my personality and worry about security for Jamie's sake. No matter what I do, some people are going to be critical, so why don't I go ahead and do what I want to do?" She released her sister's hands and pirouetted around the room again. "I'm going to Florence even if Lawrence has already married someone else! He doesn't own Florence! We'll find our own apartment, Jamie and I, and I'm going to finish that thesis finally, and Lawrence is going to help out with Jamie. It's his turn, remember."

"But will he do that?" Charlotte asked doubtfully. "I

don't want to throw cold water on your excitement, but it doesn't look as if you've thought this through carefully. Will he bother to help you if you don't live with him?''

"Yes," Nadine replied confidently. She laughed out loud. "I'm free, Char! I'm free of Everett, free of that lousy job, free of Lawrence, free of myself! It feels wonderful!''

Charlotte was still worried. "Have you talked to Lawrence about this decision?''

She shook her head. She did not want to tell Charlotte about Lily.

"Maybe you shouldn't tell Jamie until you've spoken to Lawrence. You might change your mind after talking to him, and it would only disappoint Jamie to learn you weren't going after all. He's mentioned Lawrence just about every day since he left.''

"I know. But it's too late—I've told Jamie we're leaving already. We're in this together. Life, I mean. He has to be part of my decision. If he'd been miserable at the prospect I'd have reconsidered.''

"A child that young doesn't understand decisions like these,'' Charlotte protested. "He won't learn discipline if you treat him like an adult before he can think for himself.''

Even these words did not annoy Nadine. She laughed. "You're a fine one to talk about disciplined children, Aunt Charlotte.''

Charlotte sighed. "I guess you're right. I can't manage Billy at all anymore, and Cory insists on doing everything he does. It's more than I can handle.'' She gave her sister a smile. "I'm opening a bottle of wine and we'll drink to your newfound freedom. As long as you promise you'll call Lawrence tonight.''

"Okay.'' Nadine laughed. "You know what? I'm even going to call Mom and Dad before I go.''

Charlotte's eyes widened. "Oh, Nadine. How wonderful!''

"It is about time, isn't it?'' Nadine said ruefully. "Lawrence was right.''

Charlotte dabbed at eyes that had grown moist. "Yes, he was."

Nadine gave her sister a hug, a lump in her throat also.

That night after Nadine had tucked Jamie in bed she put another call through to Lawrence.

"Dica pura?"

Lily was still there! That *must* mean she and Lawrence had reconciled! Nadine gripped the receiver.

"Hello, Lily." She kept her voice as cordial as she could. "It's Nadine again."

"Hello, Nadine." Her voice sounded deliciously sleepy and sexy. Nadine bit her lip, imagining Lawrence lying beside her in the wide bed.

"Is Lawrence there?"

Lily hesitated, then said, "I'm sorry; he is still away."

"Oh." Nadine could not tell if she was lying.

"I will tell him you called. Is there a message?"

"Yes," Nadine replied quickly. "Tell him I'm coming to Florence next week and I'll call him from the *pensione*."

"The *pensione*?"

In the background Nadine heard the distinctive sound of a man's voice. So Lily was not alone; she had lied when she said Lawrence was not there. It should not matter to her, Nadine reminded herself, for she had made the decision to move to Florence knowing that she would not be living with Lawrence, but it did matter. Tears burned her eyes. She could not bear the thought of Lily being held in his arms, in his bed.

"Goodnight," she managed to get out with difficulty, and hung up quickly.

It took over an hour to calm herself. At last she did and crawled tiredly into bed. She would have to get used to Lawrence's affairs. Eventually they would learn to deal as friends.

But she ached inside. She had wanted to be friends when

they saw each other in Florence over a month ago and she had found then that it was impossible. Her emotions went far beyond the realm of companionship and affection. They soared into another world of physical desire, dizzying adoration, consciousness of his thoughts and dreams. She was bound eternally to him. To imagine that she could live in the same city with him and pretend they were just friends was absurd.

Yet absurd though it was, she felt strong enough to try.

Chapter Twelve

❧

Ironically, the first familiar person Nadine encountered in Florence was Lily herself. She and Jamie had arrived just that morning, and after leaving their suitcases at an inexpensive *pensione* near the railway station, they went out to explore the city together. They were walking across the Ponte Vecchio, window-shopping with great delight, when Nadine glimpsed Lily coming toward them.

"It is Nadine? You look different," the throaty, accented voice called out to her cheerfully.

She was just as Nadine remembered: tall, self-confident, and gorgeous. A large white sunhat trimmed with yellow flowers covered her golden hair; a flowing yellow dress molded her slender figure. Long, scarlet-tipped fingers gleamed in the afternoon sunshine with the sweeping gestures she made as she talked. Her lips were a vivid red; her large, brown eyes were made seductively larger with the help of mascara and eyeshadow.

But although Lily had not changed outwardly, she affected Nadine differently. She seemed less large and powerful; less able to manipulate and command with a mere flash of those brilliant eyes.

"Hello, Lily."

"You have seen Lawrence?"

"Not yet. What are you doing now? Have you been in Florence all this time?"

"No, I am here on holiday." She hesitated. "I married Lorenzo three years ago."

"I know," Nadine replied calmly. "I'm sorry about the divorce. That must have been painful." She longed to ask whether she and Lawrence were together again and planned to remarry, but the words stuck in her throat.

Lily looked sad. "So, you know. We were divorced because we had no child. Lorenzo wanted a child so badly. . . ." She turned her mesmerizing gaze to Jamie, who eyed her steadily. "This is the child Lorenzo told me about, I think. How I wish he was mine."

Studying her, Nadine realized the change she saw was not in Lily but in herself. Lily had the same commanding presence and devouring loveliness; but it was Nadine who was less able to be devoured. She was not shaken by Lily's implication that Lawrence was interested in her only because of Jamie; she simply did not believe it. She was no longer intimidated by Lawrence's former wife as she would have been four years ago.

Magnanimity seeped through her, filling her with a clear, refreshing glow that made her feel lighter than air. If nothing else, she and Lily had one thing in common: They loved the same man. The jealousy and hatred she had nurtured for the woman Lawrence had chosen over her dissolved, leaving instead a wonderful sensation of empathy and relief. Lily was nice, she decided. Very nice.

"I'm glad we ran into each other," she said, and meant it. "As soon as I'm settled let's get together."

Lily rewarded Nadine's friendliness with a dazzling smile of pearly teeth. "That will be *meraviglioso*. I am only here a few days more, however. I live in Paris now. But we will talk before I leave." And with that she took her departure after another curiously sad smile at Jamie.

They returned to the *pensione* soon afterward. Nadine settled Jamie at the desk with his crayons and notepad, then picked up the telephone and dialed Lawrence's number.

He sounded curt when he heard her voice. "Where are you?"

"At the Pensione Maschella."

"How long have you been here?"

"We arrived this morning."

"Why didn't you call? I would have met you."

"I called twice from the States," she reminded him.

"I know." He sounded tired. "I've been in Rome for the past week or so, setting up for a show next February. Not a big one, but a friend's handling it and I wanted to do it."

Nadine frowned. If he had been in Rome, what was Lily doing in his villa?

"When did you get back?"

"Yesterday. I tried calling you last night, but your phone had been disconnected."

Nadine swallowed, longing for him so much that she experienced a physical ache in her chest. Was he lying to her about being in Rome?

"We'll have to get together soon," she tried. "I haven't had a chance to discuss my plans with you yet."

"Your plans?" He sounded puzzled.

"Yes." She plunged ahead hastily. "I'll need your help financially the next few weeks. Jamie and I will have to find an apartment. I hope you'll be able to take care of him while I look into the work that needs to be done on my master's, and I also have to find some kind of part-time job."

There was a heavy silence on the other end of the line.

"What's going on, Nadine?" he asked flatly. When she didn't speak he continued, "I can't wait to hear your reason for not coming straight over here and for your assuming we'll be living apart, but I don't think the telephone's the best way for me to hear it." There was a hint of anger in his voice. "Your life's your own, Nadine, and I'm the last person to try and make you do something you don't want to. But whatever your reason is, it'd better be good."

"It is."

He drew a breath. "Okay. Then let's talk about it. Dinner at my place? Jamie can sleep upstairs and we'll talk then."

She hesitated, then remembered that she might as well begin right away learning to treat him as a friend. "That would be fine."

"I'll be over in half an hour to pick you up."

Nadine replaced the receiver and went into the bathroom to take a shower. She had come to Florence for her own reasons, she reminded herself firmly, willing her tears away. She had not come here because of Lawrence. She must not allow every conversation she had with him to shatter her like this. The hot water felt good on the back of her neck. She closed her eyes.

She had slipped into a soft mauve sweater and her blue jeans and was drying her hair with a towel when Lawrence arrived.

He regarded her without speaking, then turned to Jamie, who stared with delight at his father, then ran to hug him.

"Hello, son."

"Hello."

"Done any more drawings since I saw you?"

"Yes," Jamie replied seriously. "I've been working very hard."

Lawrence smiled. "You'll show them to me as soon as we get to my place. Want to see where I live?"

Jamie nodded enthusiastically. "Mommy told me about the field and the room you draw in and the jewels—"

"Jewels?" He smiled curiously.

Nadine explained, embarrassed, "Just the dew in the field when the sun hits it in the morning."

"Ah."

"It sounds nice," Jamie added wistfully.

Lawrence's eyes were fixed on Nadine. "Let's get going," he said quietly.

They drove through the late-afternoon sunlight that gilded the coppery hills toward Fiesole. Nadine was silent, but Lawrence did more than his fair share of talking to Jamie, who eagerly asked question after question about his new home, staring wide-eyed out the window at the fleeting glimpses of cobbled streets, the river, the burnished fields.

Lawrence parked on the hill outside his villa. He put out a hand to Jamie and gave Nadine a disarming smile that made her heart skip a beat. She followed them. What was she doing, she asked herself, getting embroiled all over again in feelings for a man she knew she could not live with?

When they stepped inside the living room, Jamie took a deep breath of wonder and awe.

"Very, very, very nice," he pronounced with satisfaction. Lawrence grinned in pleasure.

"Want to look around?" he suggested, setting the bags down just inside the front door. "I'll take you on a tour. Nadine, you come too."

Meekly, she agreed, and followed them up the wide stairs. The large second floor had been divided by a walled partition. A smaller room, furnished with a twin-size bed, a wooden desk, and a cherry rug on the floor, was instantly recognized by Jamie.

"This is my room!"

Nadine gave a surprised glance to Lawrence, who was eyeing her anxiously.

"It *is* nice," she agreed.

"I'm glad you like it."

She did not know what to think.

"I'm going to show Jamie the studio." Lawrence slipped an arm around her shoulders. "Want to go downstairs and fix yourself a drink? There's cold wine in the icebox. Help yourself to whatever you'd like."

She nodded, feeling shy, and left Jamie with his father.

The serenity of the villa had cast her doubt and suspicions into a shadow. Perhaps there was some explanation. In any case, she would give Lawrence the chance to explain. Her eyes were soft when she took out the Asti Spumante from the icebox, and she noted the plate of antipasto Lawrence had prepared. Whatever his faults Lawrence was a dear man. He was generous, considerate, warmhearted. Deep love lifted her spirit as she stepped onto the patio and looked over the field in the rust light of the setting sun.

She turned around and smiled at the man and boy coming onto the patio hand in hand.

"Like it, Jamie?"

"Oh, yes!" He was too impressed for speech.

They ate a light repast on the patio: antipasto, fresh scallops, asparagus, and salad. By mutual consent they waited until Jamie went to bed before attacking their still-unresolved conflicts. Their conversation was easy and relaxed, addressed mostly to Jamie, whose questions about the country he was now in seemed endless.

Eventually his golden eyelashes grew heavy and drooped as he struggled to keep awake. Lawrence looked at Nadine and said gently:

"Tonight it's your privilege to put him to bed. I'll wash the dishes. But we'll take turns after this, okay?"

She nodded, aware as well as he that Jamie would probably want the comforting presence of his mother putting him to bed on his first night in a strange house. They rose; Lawrence picked him up, kissed his forehead, and handed him to Nadine. She carried him, half asleep in her arms, to his room.

Lawrence looked up when Nadine returned to the kitchen. "I'm almost finished." He was elbow-deep in sudsy water.

"I'll dry," Nadine offered.

"Don't bother; they'll dry by themselves. There's still some wine left. Why don't you take it onto the patio? I'll be there in a second."

She did as she was told, set the bottle on the low table outside, then perched on the low stone wall overlooking the twilight-bathed field. A tangy scent of cut grass, wild flowers, and pine trees wove its way through the quiet air, and there was a faint crispness in the fluttering breeze heralding an early winter.

Vividly she remembered the mysterious loneliness she had felt when she had last been on the patio, overlooking the same field just a month earlier. Then she had experienced an awesome yearning for her son, which somehow got entangled with a yearning for his father. It had been too confusing to bear. But tonight there was no feeling of bewilderment or mysticism. Her son was just above her, and his open window made it possible for him to hear her if she called his name. And the love that filled her chest for Lawrence barred the feeling of loneliness.

His arms wrapped around her waist as he sat down directly behind her and pulled her against his chest. She tilted her head back.

"The nightingale's back," he murmured. "I heard him last night. I hadn't heard him for months."

Nadine closed her eyes and strained her ears. Sure enough, the clear, flutelike melody floated to the villa from the woods. They shared the spellbinding moment without speaking.

One of Lawrence's fingers traced down from her throat, down her breastbone, to her abdomen, then circled around and found its way up to her underarm, across her shoulder, and back to her chin. He tilted her head back still farther so he could meet her lips with his own.

"Your heart's beating so fast," he whispered. "What are you thinking?"

In truth she had been thinking of nothing, simply hearing the heavenly melody of the songbird, breathing the fragrant air, and experiencing with pleasure the tremors in her body that his hands evoked. Was she willing to forgive his recent unfaithfulness and his lie about being in Rome simply because of the effect of his hands and breath on her body? She sighed faintly, then turned around to face him. Her gaze was filled with puzzlement and longing; he responded with a look of resentment and passion. Perhaps there was an explanation, Nadine thought again, and her heart raced.

"I was thinking about you," she breathed. "I love you. I'm afraid my heart's going to burst."

"Well, at least that's an improvement on your being afraid your heart would break if you loved me," he muttered in response. "But why in God's name don't you want to live with me if you love me?"

Aware that he was not convinced by her admission of her love, Nadine held his gaze.

"Because of Lily."

"Lily?" he barked. "What has she got to do with anything?" He rose and folded his arms forbiddingly. Nadine remained perched on the wall and dropped her eyes to the starlit tiles at her feet.

"I called twice from the States," she said steadily. "Lily answered both times. I figured you'd reconciled. But even if I can't live with you, I still want to live in Florence. There's no reason why I shouldn't. I want to finish my master's thesis. I want Jamie out of New York. It doesn't seem like such an awful thing to ask for your help in bringing up Jamie, even if we don't live together, No matter how you feel about me, I still want Jamie to be able to see you." She lifted her eyes at last and found Lawrence regarding her gravely. "What is going on between you and Lily? If you were really in Rome, why was she here?" Her voice was very low.

Lawrence sat down again.

"You don't trust me an inch, do you?" He sounded incredulous and sad. "I wonder if you ever will. Yes, I was in Rome. I can give you the phone number of the friend I was staying with if you want to ask him." He paused. "I gave Lily the keys to the villa before I left for Rome. In spite of our lousy divorce case, we've remained friends. She was in

Florence for a couple of weeks, and since I wasn't going to be here I told her she and her husband could stay there." He noticed Nadine's startled expression. "Lily married a widower, from Paris. She lives there now. He already has three children by his previous wife. She found out she couldn't have children of her own. It's been hard for her to get used to that. I hope she gets some satisfaction out of taking care of her stepchildren."

Nadine remembered the wistful tone in Lily's voice when she had said, "I wish he was mine." Now she understood the real reason for the longing in her voice, and her heart flowed out in sympathy.

Lawrence mistook her silence.

"For God's sake, I said I'd be faithful, and I have been! I will be! How am I going to get you to believe that?"

There was a long silence while Nadine struggled with a wash of emotion and relief that threatened to make her break down. She loved him so much! She gulped at her tears, then said:

"It doesn't matter if I believe you or not." Lawrence sucked in his breath in protest. Quickly she swallowed again, and held out her hands: "What I mean is, I love you so much I'll forgive anything," she explained huskily. She was trembling.

Lawrence's hands gripped hers.

"Really and truly?"

"Really and truly," she repeated after him.

"You really love me?"

She was enfolded in his arms. "Oh, Lawrence, how could I help loving you? My heart would stop beating if I didn't love you. Even when I thought you and Lily had reconciled I still wanted to be near you and to share Jamie with you."

His lips found hers. "Sweetheart," he murmured, holding her closer to him. "You've no idea how good it is to hear you say that. How I've missed you!"

Their lips met.

"You know something?" Nadine declared, drawing away slightly. "I feel so awake! So alive! I feel I've awoken from one of those endlessly confusing, emotional dreams that leave you exhausted. I'm in control again! I can run, I can fly—"

He broke in, pulling her to his chest. "You won't fly from me again, will you?"

"I love you so much that I couldn't fly from you ever!" she said passionately. "I'll forgive even the unforgivable things you do, that's how much I love you!"

Laughter bubbled up and spilled over in an entrancing gurgle. Lawrence smiled.

"I won't say I won't do something unforgivable sometime," he said seriously, however. "But I'll try my damndest not to."

Their lips joined again, and as the kiss deepened Nadine felt rippling tremors of joy and excitement coursing through her. She explored the familiar row of teeth, the roof of his mouth, the faint fruity taste of wine on his tongue. She could feel the hard evidence of his arousal as she pressed against him, nibbling his ear.

"We'll get married next week," he said hoarsely, when she had unbuttoned his shirt and her soft teeth had found an erect nipple. One hand tugged her hair and another explored her ribs, her underarm, her breast.

"We will," she stopped to breathe, then lost herself in his mouth again.

After a while he protested softly, "We can't do this out here. What if Jamie wakes up?" But as her hand reached for his belt buckle he gave a faint groan.

"Jamie's got a heavy dose of jet lag, in addition to having been up for about twelve hours straight. He'll sleep like a log for at least twelve hours more. Besides, we can't go in now. It's too heavenly out here. Can you smell the pines? The poppies? I'm delirious, Lawrence. . . ."

He lifted her to her feet and they made their way to the low couch. Before they had reached it he took off her thin cotton sweater. She wore nothing underneath. He stood before her, drinking in her loveliness bathed in starlight and scented by the fragrant fall air. Even in the dusk she discerned the light of love and desire in his eyes for her alone.

"How I love you," he murmured huskily, lowering himself beside her and covering her smooth, silvery body with his own while the nightingale in the woods broke out into unearthly song again.

RAPTURE ROMANCE

*Provocative and sensual,
passionate and tender—
the magic and mystery of love
in all its many guises*

NEW Titles Available Now   (0451)

23☐**MIDNIGHT EYES by Deborah Benêt.** Noble was as wary of Egyptian men as Talat was of American career women. Could their passion burn through the cultures that bound them?
(124766—$1.95)*

24☐**DANCE OF DESIRE by Elizabeth Allison.** Jeffery Northrop offered dancer Patrice Edwards love beyond her wildest dreams—but could she give up her hard-won independence in exchange?
(124774—$1.95)*

25☐**PAINTED SECRETS by Ellie Winslow.** He'd left her four years ago, but now Lawrence Stebbing was back. For Nadine's love—or their son?
(124782—$1.95)*

26☐**STRANGERS WHO LOVE by Sharon Wagner.** Was Paul Roarke really an easily bought-off fortune-hunter? Arianna didn't think so, until her new husband suddenly disappeared . . .
(124790—$1.95)*

*Price is $2.25 in Canada

**Buy them at your local bookstore or use
coupon on next page for ordering.**

RAPTURE ROMANCE

Provocative and sensual, passionate and tender— the magic and mystery of love in all its many guises

RAPTURE ROMANCE

*Provocative and sensual,
passionate and tender—
the magic and mystery of love
in all its many guises*

Coming next month

FROSTFIRE by Jennifer Dale. Rachel Devlin thought she only wanted revenge on womanizer Colin Knight. But once she found herself in his arms, her fury turned to desire . . .

PRECIOUS POSSESSION by Kathryn Kent. There was a strength in Max Randolph to which Sabrina Whitfield couldn't help responding. But something warned her to beware, for this ambitious businessman was also her arch rival . . .

STARDUST AND DIAMONDS by JoAnn Robb. Brilliant astronomer Althea Thorne had her gaze fixed on the heavens until baseball star Matt Powers eclipsed all else. But Althea worried that their different worlds would collide and destroy their love . . .

HEART'S VICTORY by Laurel Chandler. Karen Meredith pledged no man would come between her and ballet, until champion skier Erik Nylund melted her icy resistance. But would she have to sacrifice her career for love?

A SHARED LOVE by Elisa Stone. Mark Hager awakened Courtney to an ecstasy she had denied herself. But then she discovered Mark's secret, a secret that could destroy her dreams of love . . .

FORBIDDEN JOY by Nina Coombs. Dynamic physicist Stephen Blackford helped cool New Englander Hester Mather blossom into a confident, beautiful woman. Then he was gone, leaving her to question his love—and to wonder whether the new woman she'd become could win him back. . . .

TELL US YOUR OPINIONS AND RECEIVE A FREE COPY OF THE RAPTURE NEWSLETTER.

Thank you for filling out our questionnaire. Your response to the following questions will help us to bring you more and better books. In appreciation of your help we will send you a free copy of the Rapture Newsletter.

1. Book Title:_____

   Book #:_____ (5-7)

2. Using the scale below how would you rate this book on the following features? Please write in one rating from 0-10 for each feature in the spaces provided. Ignore bracketed numbers.

(Poor) 0 1 2 3 4 5 6 7 8 9 10 (Excellent)
                                      0-10 Rating

Overall Opinion of Book............... _____ (8)
Plot/Story......................... _____ (9)
Setting/Location...................... _____ (10)
Writing Style......................... _____ (11)
Dialogue............................ _____ (12)
Love Scenes......................... _____ (13)
Character Development:
Heroine:............................ _____ (14)
Hero:.............................. _____ (15)
Romantic Scene on Front Cover.......... _____ (16)
Back Cover Story Outline .... _____ (17)
First Page Excerpts................... _____ (18)

3. What is your: Education: Age:_____(20-22)

      High School ( )1   4 Yrs. College ( )3
      2 Yrs. College ( )2   Post Grad   ( )4 (23)

4. Print Name:_____

   Address:_____

   City:_____State:_____Zip:_____

   Phone # ( )_____(25)

Thank you for your time and effort. Please send to New American Library, Rapture Romance Research Department, 1633 Broadway, New York, NY 10019.

SPECIAL $1.00 REBATE OFFER
WHEN YOU BUY
FOUR RAPTURE ROMANCES

To receive your cash refund, send:

1. This coupon: To qualify for the $1.00 refund, this coupon, completed with your name and address, must be used. (Certificate may not be reproduced)

2. Proof of purchase: Print, on the reverse side of this coupon, the *title* of the books, the *numbers* of the books (on the upper right hand of the front cover preceding the price), and the U.P.C. numbers (on the back covers) on your next four purchases.

3. Cash register receipts, with prices circled to:
   Rapture Romance $1.00 Refund Offer
   P.O. Box NB037
   El Paso, Texas 79977

Offer good only in the U.S. and Canada. Limit one refund/response per household for any group of four Rapture Romance titles. Void where prohibited, taxed or restricted. Allow 6–8 weeks for delivery. Offer expires March 31, 1984.

NAME_____

ADDRESS_____

CITY_____STATE_____ZIP_____

SPECIAL $1.00 REBATE OFFER
WHEN YOU BUY
FOUR RAPTURE ROMANCES

See complete details on reverse

1. Book Title _____

   Book Number 451-_____

   U.P.C. Number 7116200195-_____

2. Book Title _____

   Book Number 451-_____

   U.P.C. Number 7116200195-_____

3. Book Title _____

   Book Number 451-_____

   U.P.C. Number 7116200195-_____

4. Book Title _____

   Book Number 451-_____

   U.P.C. Number 7116200195-_____

—— U.P.C. Number

0

SAMPLE

71162 00195